"Thank you ⟨⟨⟨ his, no longer ⟨⟨⟨ ⟨⟨⟨ energy that sang along her skin where they touched. He leaned in, dipping his chin.**

Is he going to kiss me?

God, she wanted him to, wanted to know what he tasted like and what his hands felt like tangled in her hair. She was surprised by the pulsing need thrumming beneath her rib cage.

But—

She forced herself to picture Rachel's smile, the one in the picture she'd sent Sorcha after her elopement with Patrick. When that didn't work, Sorcha reminded herself about her no-strings-no-hurt mantra.

But what if...what if we just spent the night together? Would that really be so bad?

Is he a man you can spend one night with and call it good? What about his daughter? The fact he was once Rachel's husband? Could you ignore all those things?

As he leaned closer, only the scent of hospital soap and something so wonderfully masculine separating their bodies, she thought she might like to find out.

Dear Reader,

Fáilte. I hope you brought tissues for this one! This was more than a romance novel for me; this was a love letter to Ireland, to second chances that light up our darkest moments and to harlequin Great Danes, one of whom stole our hearts in real life.

I'm thrilled to share Patrick and Sorcha's love story with you. Patrick isn't quick to love—he's played that game and lost (so darn relatable). Sorcha is even more closed off after the childhood she endured. In her mind, family means something that can be taken from you and she won't take that risk again.

Or will she? This story was fun to write because I saw so much love brimming just underneath the terrified surfaces of my characters. Teasing that out was a challenge, but one that I hope paid off. In this second-chance, single-dad romance, there is a little bit of all of us, I think—our fears and insecurities around love, sure, but also our joys and connections and the families we build when we need support the most.

Drop me a line and let me know what you think on X, Instagram or Facebook, or by email at kristinelynnauthor@gmail.com.

Kristine

A KISS WITH THE IRISH SURGEON

KRISTINE LYNN

MEDICAL ROMANCE

Harlequin®
MEDICAL
ROMANCE

ISBN-13: 978-1-335-94288-3

A Kiss with the Irish Surgeon

Recycling programs
for this product may
not exist in your area.

Harlequin Enterprises ULC
22 Adelaide St. West, 41st Floor
Toronto, Ontario M5H 4E3, Canada
www.Harlequin.com

Printed in U.S.A.

Books by Kristine Lynn

Harlequin Medical Romance

Brought Together by His Baby
Accidentally Dating His Boss
Their Six-Month Marriage Ruse

Visit the Author Profile page at Harlequin.com.

To Patrick and George.

Your time together was never going to be long enough. This book is my way of saying thank you for the love you've given Iz and I.

CHAPTER ONE

PATRICK QUINN STARED at the suitcase. It wasn't even half full, and yet he couldn't imagine a single other item he wanted to pack. A glance at his mostly empty closet confirmed the unease growing in his chest, then spread from limb to limb like a phantom illness.

Rachel's things were gone by now, donated to a women's shelter where they'd be loved and appreciated. But even his side of the walk-in closet haunted him.

The shirts were his, technically, but she'd bought them, citing his horrible fashion sense. So, they'd stay. He could buy new shirts in the States.

The scarf in County Kerry's colors she'd bought him as an anniversary present still smelled like her. Yeah, that was going to the shelter next.

And the stethoscope? Something he used every day at work as the head oncology surgeon at St. Michael's Hospital? He should pack it—the tool was still in great condition and buying another was a pointless expense. But an image of his late wife wearing it—and nothing else, a present to him the

day he'd become a surgical general practitioner—
was one more ghost chasing him out of the life
they'd built together.

No. This move was a fresh start from every
angle. Everything must go.

Because it wasn't an invisible plague haunting
him day and night until he'd had no choice but to
take the job in Boston in the hopes of quieting it.
The memory of his wife was a very real thing, and
it was everywhere. While that had been a good
thing at first—comforting, even—now it held him
hostage, refusing to let him move on.

And he was ready to move on. The irony that it
was Rachel's last request before nurses had moved
into their home wasn't lost on him. He ran a hand
along the only item of hers he was taking with them
across the Atlantic as she'd requested—her ashes
in a simple silver urn she'd picked out on their last
weekend together.

It should have been, if not a happy weekend, at
least a peaceful one with lunch at their favorite pub.
But that day three years ago, they'd walked by a fu-
neral home and Rachel, clad in a headscarf to hide
her chemo-ravaged hair, had insisted they go in.

There, in front of a dozen choices of receptacles
they were supposed to choose from to put her remains in, she'd held his hand and issued words no
husband should have to hear.

"I want you and Aoife to be happy, Patrick. And
that means letting me go."

"I can't," he'd sobbed into her frail arms. The

morbid urns and caskets and smell of death had almost suffocated him. Even now, he could still smell that room where it'd finally hit him—his wife would die and he'd be left behind to raise their infant daughter alone. "I promised to love you forever."

"No." She'd smiled, her lips cracked and dry from the chemo, "you promised you'd love me all my life, and that's over now. It's not going to do you any good to mourn me like Miss Havisham, love. Make a life for you and our daughter and bring me home to my parents."

"You *are* home," he'd whispered into her paper-thin skin that smelled of chemicals.

"She needs to meet them, Patrick. No matter what my parents said about you, about me, about us, they deserve to know their grandchild and say goodbye to me."

He'd choked on a half sob, half grunt of disapproval.

"I mean it. Aoife's only got you and her precious innocence to help her grieve. Give my parents the chance to help." He'd nodded, but she must have seen through it. She'd poked his chest. "So help me, if you sit around Dublin moping, I'll haunt you."

Patrick put the urn in his backpack and sighed. It was strange to think that soon, he wouldn't have it anymore.

"Oh, darling, you haunt me still," he whispered into the room he'd say goodbye to for the next nine months, if not forever. Maybe when he got home after the interim chief of surgery contract in Boston was up, Rachel's ghost would be gone. Or maybe he'd sell this place so he'd feel less guilty for moving on when she still seemed to be everywhere. But his American bride had been right about one thing—it was better for him and Aoife both to move forward with their lives.

He'd loved and lost, but that happened to people every day—he saw it in the hospital waiting room more often than he dared to admit.

What mattered most was caring for Aoife, who he loved as much as life itself. This temporary move would be good for them both.

"Da!" a small but mighty voice called out. He smiled. His little love was awake, finally. They had to head to the airport in less than two hours. *"Da!"*

"I'm coming, love," he called out.

He strode down the hallway and turned the corner into what he could only describe as chaos, plain and simple. "What's going on here, *mo grá*?" he asked, pointing to the pile of dresses and shoes at the foot of his daughter's bed.

"My clothes for the trip," Aoife said, putting a piece of paper on the top.

"I packed for you, love. Your suitcase is already in my room. Now clean this up before Mamó comes to pick us up. We don't have much time and you still need to eat."

"Da," Aoife said, her hands on her hips as if she commanded all of the European Union and not only his attention. "You packed my trousers and sweaters and nothin' pretty."

He saved a chuckle from escaping his throat. He'd run surgical programs, trained field medics, lived on two continents and still his daughter eluded him.

"I'm sorry. An oversight, I assure you."

"Okay. But I still need these. Put them in the case?" she asked. "Puhleease?" His daughter's smile was one more reminder of Rachel he was taking overseas. This one, he'd pack happily.

"I'll toss them in," he said, picking up a few. The slip of paper fell and he caught it midair.

"What's this?" he asked, reading it over. He marveled at the words that were actually legible, if he read them phonetically. Mamó, his mom, studied with Aoife on the days she didn't have preschool and was working wonders on Aoife's reading and writing. That, and her uncanny way of making him forget she was barely four every time she spoke, would serve her well in America.

"A list for the fairies," she replied, tossing her crimson ringlets over her shoulder. "I asked them for things I really, *really* want since it's almost St. Patrick's Day, but then I got to thinking…"

She pointed at the dresses in Patrick's arms, a frown on her pouty little lips. "What if they don't know where I'm going?"

He tried to keep up. Fairies had been Rachel and Aoife's thing, hers and Mamó's after that. He preferred the grounded world of medicine where every ailment had a cure, each injury a treatment plan.

"I'm sure they've got a network of fairy friends who will track you as we travel," he said. That obviously wasn't the right answer given the way her brows pulled in at the center.

"They're not *Santa*, Da. They don't have elves. I know the fairies here, and I want them to remember what I asked for in case they can't fly over the ocean." God, she was growing like a primrose in spring. Her sass and intelligence were growing faster.

Patrick glanced over the list.

P-u-p-y was written on the top. "You want a dog?" he asked.

She nodded. "Like Susan and Clara down the hill. They don't let me pet their wee thing anymore so I want my own."

His chest ached under the weight of all he couldn't give his daughter. Hopefully what he could—love, financial security, a life of stability—would be enough.

"We'll talk about it when we're back. Dogs don't travel well in the belly of a plane."

The pout grew. Fascinating that women learned the skill at such a young age. He chuckled until his gaze fell to the item at the bottom of the list, a star by it, indicating its importance.

"A new ma?" he asked. His chest now felt like an anvil was sitting on it. Cardiac arrest wasn't common in men in their late thirties, but it wasn't impossible, either. He rubbed at the area absently as he thought through how to answer.

"That's a tough one for the fairies to tackle, Aoife," he started. Hopefully she wouldn't notice the catch in his throat. "A ma is something that isn't just dropped from the heavens into our laps."

Strictly speaking, that wasn't entirely true. Rachel had, in fact, fallen into his lap at O'Shanahan's Irish pub in South Boston when a billiards player had knocked into her. She'd always claimed it was fairies that had led her to him just as he finished his residency and was moving home to Dublin to start at St. Michael's.

He cleared his throat. "I had to work hard to find the one that brought you into this world, and it would take a lot more work to find another." That part was true.

"Well, I'm leavin' it on there!" Aoife exclaimed. She picked up a pretty dress. "You hafta go, Da. I need to change. Mamó says real princesses don't wear tights to fly."

Her small body corralled him toward the door before she shut him on the other side of it.

He sighed, still holding the list in his hand, which shook. Not a good look for a doctor taking on a chief of surgery position.

A new ma.

The words rubbed like sandpaper down his heart, agitating it.

It wasn't like he hadn't thought about starting to date, or inviting someone else into his and Aoife's lives. He had, and the idea sent a whisper of a thrill coursing through his blood. But then it would meet with the almost crippling guilt blocking the entrance to his heart, and he would abandon the idea. He had to care for Aoife; that was the most important thing.

But now... Well, he couldn't be sure her list wasn't a prescription for how to do just that.

Too bad they were bound for Boston, the one place he'd sworn he'd never return to. Too much damage over too long a time to think of it as anything other than a means to an end. He'd bring Rachel's ashes home to America, then be done. Which meant, even if Aoife's list made sense, nothing permanent could happen there—not a puppy, and certainly not a woman in their lives. But when they got back to Ireland, he'd make an effort to put some thought into what was best for him and Aoife moving forward. Even dating.

Will you be ready by then?

Thankfully, the interim chief job was for a full nine months—enough time to figure that out. And to help an old friend who'd mentored him in medical school cover a position while the actual chief took her maternity leave, introduce Aoife to her grandparents and say a final goodbye to Rachel, who wouldn't be making the trip back to Dublin with them.

How could she, when her mother and father desperately wanted their girl back home, the girl they claimed he'd stolen from them? He owed them that, at least. It'd been impossible for him to come with her when Rachel visited each year—until she'd gotten sick. Not just because he'd never been welcome—which he hadn't. But because he'd been dedicated to his career for too many years. He'd thought he'd have plenty of time with Rachel after he'd gotten ahead at work, but time was the one thing life hadn't given them.

Now, he needed to make things right and honor his late wife's wishes by bringing her ashes home. He might have failed Rachel in a thousand other ways, but this one thing—giving her back to her parents—he could do. If only it didn't mean going back to Boston, where it'd all begun. In that way, nine months was an eternity.

But then he and his daughter could start their lives over, this trip finally behind them. It was enough to make a widower feel a little hope blossoming in places where light rarely shone.

"Boston, I hope you're ready for us," he whispered. He pulled up the airline tickets and patted the pocket on his backpack, making sure the passports were there.

He'd feel a whole lot better if this trip wasn't happening on St. Patty's Day, the day he'd met his future wife a decade earlier.

"Aoife," he called back. "Let's get going. If you can hurry, *mo grá*, I'll stop at Liam's for a cranberry scone."

She squealed and shouted, "I'm coming, Da, but my clothes—"

"Leave 'em," he shouted back, slinging his backpack over his shoulder and grabbing the cases in his free hands. In the kitchen, he left a note for the housekeeper to start with Aoife's room once they'd left. It felt odd, leaving the place where Aoife was born, where she'd taken her first steps, where her mother took her final breath.

But the sooner they left, the sooner they could say a final goodbye to Rachel, then hurry back to their side of the pond and leave America—with its own brand of tragic memories—behind for good.

CHAPTER TWO

SORCHA KELLY STARED into the glass of Jameson whiskey, wishing it had the power to reflect something other than her solitary image back at her. The raucous music blaring from the speakers was in direct opposition to her mood. Give her a maudlin ballad instead.

Even today. *Especially* today.

The crowd grew in size and noise, their celebratory cries of *"Sláinte!"* reaching a crescendo as soon as the fire marshal popped in to say they'd reached capacity.

Sorcha smiled and took the shot in a single swallow. The more things changed, the more they stayed the same. She waved at Kellan, the fire marshal who'd pulled the short straw that year. No one wanted cops and fire personnel in uniform, not on St. Patty's Day. They'd drink for free in plain clothes, but in uniform? They were the enemy of fun.

He waved back, an improvement from last year when he'd flipped her off.

It wasn't her fault. She'd turned him down kindly

enough. She just didn't have the time or heart for a guy in her life, not that she expected him to understand. To her, a family meant inevitable loss and heartache, a lesson hammered into her during her own childhood. Her parents had never gotten over the loss of Sorcha's sister, which begged the question of why she'd willingly invite that kind of pain into her life. Especially when she could work at a hospital and save other families from experiencing that loss instead.

It really wasn't a question—she never wanted to put her heart ahead of her work, no matter how nice guys like Kellan O'Connor were, or how much her parents tried to convince her to put work aside and honor her Irish Catholic ways.

Right. The Irish Catholic ways.

Marry, breed, fight, drink, and then start the whole process over again. She'd been told by more than one of her fellow first-generation Irish American friends that going against the grain was like turning your back on the sea—highly dangerous and bound to take you under eventually.

So far, she'd escaped the trappings of a tethered life, but she worried she'd have to turn around and face the storm sooner or later.

She tapped the bar.

"You having another? Aren't you usually out as soon as Kellan or one of his comrades comes around?" Sam, the bartender, asked. He was the only Scottish man allowed behind the bar of the Irish pub run by three generations of O'Shanahans, thanks to his luck at falling in love with an O'Shanahan daughter. He also knew what drew Sorcha out each St. Patty's Day, and how drastically her mission to get obliterated once a year differed from everyone else in the bar's.

Rachel. Sorcha shook her head so the ghost of her dead best friend would leave her alone. She didn't normally drink—no time for it when her sole focus was getting her clinical trial up and running. But St. Patty's Day was different. St. Patty's Day was hers and Rachel's, and Sorcha didn't see a need to find a new way of coping with Rachel's loss, or her best friend's betrayal ten years earlier that made the loss even more acute.

Whiskey did the trick just fine.

"Yup. One more and I'm out. Big day tomorrow."

"Bigger day than today? Isn't this ten years since—"

"It is." Sorcha waved him off, her head a little light from the booze and the proximity of so many screaming banshees dancing behind her on O'Shanahan's small linoleum dance floor. Their joy was palpable. Annoyingly so. "But it doesn't matter. Mick's giving his speech tomorrow at the hospital. It's finally happening."

"Congrats," Sam said. He grabbed a glass, poured himself a shot of whiskey and topped hers off. "To your trial finally getting funded."

They clinked glasses and both tossed back the amber liquid at the same time.

Sorcha hissed. Whiskey was a fine way to forget, but she didn't do it often enough to make it burn less.

"*Sláinte,*" she said, putting her empty glass on the bar with far less enthusiasm than the giggling women next to her. An image of her and Rachel in those same seats, similar smiles on their faces, almost suffocated her. "So, what's the craic, Sam?"

"Not much. Kiera's up walking and said her first word."

"Lemme guess—*da*?"

"Nope. *Ma.* I lost that bet." They laughed and it felt good to do that again, on St. Patty's Day no less. "Speaking of the guy," Sam said, pointing to a table behind her and she squinted.

The crowd was thinner by the tables—no one wanted to sit when dancing and drinking was the name of the game. But the combination of self-pity and alcohol had caught up to her, and everything farther than her hand was blurry.

"Speaking of who?" she asked Sam.

"Mick. Isn't that him?"

"Mick?" she asked. Surprise twisted her lips. But yeah, there he was—her boss, Dr. Michael O'Shea, who ran Boston General's medical program, in South Boston at a dive bar, alone.

"Dr. Kelly?" her boss replied. The formality of his address didn't sound right with the steady hum of joviality in the background. "I didn't know you lived in South Boston."

He looked less surprised and more...*guilty*?

Someone started a round of "Drunken Sailor"

and the rest of the bar—everyone but her and her boss, locked in a staring stalemate—joined in.

She shook her head, and a wave of dizziness crashed over her. The chorus of voices thrummed against her chest and she recalled another reason she didn't drink—she didn't like bars, didn't like the way they dulled her senses. As a surgeon, and a research surgeon at that, she couldn't afford to dull anything.

"I don't," she shouted over the music. "I come here every year for a friend." Her throat was raw from the whiskey. She'd feel this tomorrow. Oh, well, all she had to do was give the speech to her new staff, a speech she could repeat on no sleep or food, half-drowned in whiskey. She'd been rehearsing it since Dr. Collins had announced her maternity leave.

Boston General Hospital would need an interim chief of surgery for nine months, and Sorcha needed a way to get her trial in front of the hospital's board of directors without waiting in line behind the other ambitious doctors with billion-dollar medical innovations to pitch. Only a certain amount of funding was reserved for trials, and she wanted in. *Needed* in.

They'd *have* to listen to the interim chief's proposal, and so she'd aimed to get the chief gig no matter what. She was indispensable to Mick now, and, according to Mick's assistant who liked the Irish scones Sorcha had been baking her for years, the job was all but hers.

She just needed to formally accept it tomorrow.

"Must be some friend," Mick said, fiddling with the paper sticker on his beer bottle.

"She was," Sorcha whispered. "The best. But we had a falling out."

"Over a guy?"

Sorcha smiled, but it felt as weak as the rest of her. "Sort of. She was supposed to meet me to move into my apartment at CUNY School of Medicine, but called to tell me she was moving to Dublin with a man she'd just met. Here at this bar, actually. It was the only St. Patty's Day I couldn't make our annual date. She…she didn't even say goodbye."

The memory of her best friend's face over video chat three months later, when she'd finally called Sorcha to apologize, a ring on her finger, was etched on Sorcha's mind. Rachel had been happy, and in return, Sorcha had been cruel and unforgiving. Rachel was the only one who knew what med school meant to Sorcha, how hard it was to do it without family support. And still, her best friend had done what mattered to her, and forgotten all about Sorcha.

They'd seen each other with their other girlfriends each St. Patty's Day Rachel had flown home to visit, but it was never the same as it'd been before, when the two women had been inseparable.

The thing was, it wasn't just Rachel's fault. Ten years of maturity and therapy, and Sorcha knew she wasn't responsible for Rachel's choices, just as Rachel wasn't responsible for Sorcha's. Still…

The guilt over all the things Sorcha should have said that night Rachel had called to say she was leaving for Dublin replayed on a tortuous reel.

Come home.

Do you even know who this man is?

I miss you.

I'm sorry.

Each year on St. Patrick's Day, she gave in to the spiraling thoughts and guilt for one night. She'd wallow, then suck it up, put her head down and work through it the rest of the year.

"I'm sorry to hear that. I hope you two have mended things," Mick said. He kept glancing at the door. She followed his gaze, somehow surprised at how she could feel such despair while the rest of the patrons with slung arms around one another seemed…happy. Or at least carefree in a way Sorcha had never been.

"She died before we could."

The rest of Sorcha's pain was a result of never making the flight to Ireland, not even when Rachel got sick. At first, Sorcha had blamed this guy— Patrick, who she'd never met—for taking her best friend away, but the truth was, it was Rachel's wild temperament that led her to Dublin, to saying no to treatment when she got pregnant. And it was Sorcha's own Irish stubbornness that kept her feet firmly planted in Boston instead of putting that all aside when her friend needed her.

Because of that, she'd still never met her best friend's daughter. She couldn't only fault her friend's widowered husband for that. But she *could* despise him for not forcing Rachel to get treatment.

If he was the doctor he was supposed to be, shouldn't he have saved his own *wife*?

She shook her head. No use dragging that all back into the present again. Rachel was gone and that was that.

"Anyway, what are you doing here, sir?"

Without your wife, she wanted to add, but thankfully, the whiskey's effects on her hadn't included sassing her boss.

He bit his bottom lip and she frowned. Mick was nervous.

"I'm…meeting a friend."

Sorcha's brows went up. She liked Mick, respected him. But she liked Mick's wife, Aisling, even more. The woman was one part doting wife and mother, two parts Irish smart-ass.

"Mick—"

He put up a hand, stopping her from blurting out the accusation swelling on her tongue.

"There he is now."

"He?" Sorcha asked.

Her head whipped around to follow Mick's gaze, and the effects made her dizzier. Backlit by the spotlights on the dance floor, she couldn't make out any features, save the broad shoulders and strong silhouette of the guy heading toward them, parting the throngs of laughing people as if he were one of the ancient Irish gods.

Mick wasn't at the bar to meet another woman at least.

So, why the shroud of secrecy?

A few paces away, the dim lights over the tables took over, illuminating the stranger's face. His jaw was set, strong, and his lips unsmiling. She got the impression that he was as unenthusiastic about being out on St. Patty's Day as her. But that's where the similarities between them ended.

He was tall where she was short, impeccably dressed in a tailored button-down and slacks that hugged thick ropey muscles while she wore tights, trainers and a baggy Celtics hoodie.

His emerald green eyes were hard, as if life had dealt him a rough hand. She'd had a tough time of it, too, but still found joy where she could. She, at least, knew how to smile.

And speaking of his lips…they were flat, pressed tight, but full. Her throat was suddenly too dry. She swallowed as the stranger's stony gaze landed on her.

There was one more similarity, something that nagged at her, tugged at a memory deeply buried in her subconscious. He was Irish—she'd bet on it.

But it was something else, too.

"Dr. Quinn," Mick said, standing and ignoring the stranger's outstretched hand and opting for a tight embrace instead. "Glad you made it safely."

Then she saw it. The eyes, lips and name coming together in one real-life package. She'd seen photos of this man—photos she'd tried to forget—but the in-person version was far more damning.

They clearly hadn't done enough justice to the power in his gaze.

"Quinn?" Sorcha asked. Three shots of alcohol in less than an hour had slowed her cognitive responses, but her mind finally caught up. "Like Dr. *Patrick* Quinn?"

Her pulse raced as the man's gaze took her in, from her sneakers to her long red—and unwashed— hair pulled back into a messy ponytail.

"Yes. And you are?"

The Irish brogue meant he wasn't just Irish by heritage, but flown-in-from-Dublin Irish. Sorcha rolled her shoulders back, attempting to look strong despite her disheveled appearance. She wavered on her feet, but steadied herself as she squared off with the interloper.

"I'm Sorcha Kelly. I'm sure you've heard the name before."

A shadow passed over Patrick's face, but otherwise his lack of reaction said it all; she'd been as unimportant to her best friend's husband as she'd been to her best friend in the end.

"Rachel's best friend," Patrick said, nodding. His accent was like home, the way he said *Ray-chel* warming her from the inside out like a cup of tea with soda bread by the hearth. She shook the familiar feeling off.

Especially since the man represented everything about the home that had been stolen from her.

"I didn't know you two knew each other," Mick said. "Well," he laughed, "that'll save me an introduction."

"Mick," Sorcha said, keeping her eyes on the stranger in front of her. "Can I get a moment with your *friend*?"

Mick's aversion to confrontation won out over his obvious confusion at the situation unfolding in front of him. "I'll see about getting some food while you two catch up."

He walked away and the veil of pleasantries dropped. A dancer bumped into her, laughing and uncaring—a minor inconvenience compared to *Patrick. Here.*

Anger rose up like bile in Sorcha's throat.

Why was he here, now, talking to *her* boss in *her* bar on *her* continent?

"Yes," she said, finally addressing Patrick. "I was Rachel's best friend. Though after you stole her from me ten years ago, there wasn't much of a friendship left."

"I'm sorry," he said. Two words she'd waited a lifetime to hear, now fell flat. His emerald green eyes appeared to be lit from within and their gaze bore into Sorcha's chest, carving out the place she'd buried her grief. "I told her to come back more often, that she didn't need to worry about the money—we could afford it."

Sorcha grumbled dismissively.

"You don't get to be sorry. Not now. You should have been sorry enough to bring her home yourself, to have a wedding here where she could have had her family involved. Or sorry enough to make her fight for her life when she got sick." Sorcha was breathing heavily, the anger and grief mixing with the cheery background noise and the impossibility of seeing this man here, now.

Her head was woozy. She really should have had dinner, but she'd come straight from the hospital, a breakthrough in the lab more important than a sandwich. Now, regret came swift. She held the table for support.

"You're right," was all Patrick said, his strong—and frankly, attractive as all get out—shoulders stiff. "Everything you said is spot-on and I live with the regret every day."

Sorcha rocked back on her heels, surprised at his admission, at the realization that this man—who she'd imagined being tough and unfeeling like her Irish father—was a man grieving, too. It didn't fix how Sorcha felt, though. Didn't erase the past decade of needing her best friend since Sorcha's family couldn't champion her career in medicine, not when they'd worked their whole lives to keep their girls out of hospitals—or at least the daughter they'd cared for most.

Cara.

"What the hell are you doing here?" she finally asked. Exhaustion replaced the anger. It didn't matter that Patrick was here, only that he skipped back to his side of the pond as soon as possible.

That used to be your side of the pond, too.

She ignored her sober conscience.

She held up her hand as he opened his mouth to answer.

"You know what? It doesn't matter. I've got a big day tomorrow where I'll finally get a chance to do what Rachel and I used to dream about, and I don't need you distracting me from what really matters."

"And what is that?" Patrick asked. He leaned in, curious. As if the rest of the partygoers were turned to mute, she only saw the man in front of her. Everything, and everyone faded into the background, as if it was the middle of the day in her lab, not the heart of St. Patty's Day revelry.

Maybe it was the barrel of whiskey floating in her bloodstream, maybe it was having someone ask about her work after doing everything on her own for so long, maybe it was the scent of Irish tweed and coconut oil that had her answering against her better judgment.

"I'm going to be interim chief of surgery at the hospital I work at, and then I'll get to make my sister's death count for something." She held her breath as he leaned closer, his furrowed brows and parted lips a heady combination for a woman whose work drew limited interest from people. She continued, "I spent my childhood watching my parents say goodbye to one child and neglecting the one they still had, all while I watched my sister waste away from a brain tumor. Rachel was my best friend and supported me going to med school then surgical residency so I could find a way to save other kids with my sister's kind of tumor."

Why was she telling him all this?

Because he's safe. He doesn't know you, doesn't live here, can't judge you. And he deserves to know what he took from you when he stole Rachel away.

"And you have? Found a way to do that?"

Sorcha nodded, the realization that she was so close to her dream coming true hitting her with more force than the whiskey.

"I just need to get the clinical trial off the ground." Patrick smiled, and it broke whatever hold he'd had over her. At the same time, the party picked up in noise, a reminder of where she was and *why*. It might be a celebration to everyone else, but to Sorcha, tonight was a wake. "Anyway, I don't know why you're here and frankly, I don't give a damn. You stopped mattering to me the minute you let Rachel die."

"Dr. Kelly!" Sorcha whipped her head around, and her lips twisted in embarrassment. She hadn't seen Mick return with drinks. "That's no way to talk to Dr. Quinn. He's going to be your—"

"Colleague," Patrick interrupted, as he accepted a pint of beer from Mick. The men clinked glasses, the sound shrill to Sorcha's ears. "At Boston General. I start tomorrow, actually." He turned to Mick while Sorcha stared, wondering if she'd heard him right. Praying she hadn't.

Sorcha's mouth fell open. "No. You—you can't."

She was so close to getting everything she'd

worked for and he—he'd distract her from that. She wasn't sure how, but the swirl of emotions she'd kept under lock and key all this time said enough; he was a part of her past she wanted to keep buried.

Mick frowned. "He can and he is. He and his daughter are welcome here, and we'll all make sure they feel that way. Dr. Kelly, I suggest you go home and sober up before we announce it tomorrow."

His daughter…

Rachel's daughter was there, in Boston. A sob built in Sorcha's chest.

"I—I can't do this. I'm sorry."

With that, her fortitude finally gave in. She turned her back on the man she hated more than anyone else on the planet and ran out of O'Shanahan's, long overdue tears finally falling and chilling her skin in the cold, March air.

She didn't care what Mick thought of her outburst, whether Patrick Quinn felt welcome or not. Only erasing these feelings—guilt, loss, and fear—mattered.

So much for the magic of St. Patty's Day. Tonight, it only felt like a curse.

CHAPTER THREE

SORCHA WINCED. There wasn't much sun this time of year in Boston, but what there was shone like a spotlight onto where she was sprawled out on top of her comforter.

Her head pulsed, partly from the aftereffects of her overindulgence, partly because she was recalling the previous night's events.

Her boss had witnessed her in a sweatshirt and totally drunk the night before she was supposed to accept a promotion from him.

Then... *Oh, then.* Patrick Quinn in the flesh. On her continent. In *her* dive bar, in the middle of *her* annual pity session. And who was slated to start working at *her* hospital that morning. At least she'd be his boss and could schedule him as far from her as possible.

Then maybe she could forget his worst offense, the one that Sorcha had thought about day and night the past few years. Patrick Quinn, renowned surgical oncologist, had let his wife die of cancer without doing everything in his power to convince her to consider treatment.

He may have lost a spouse, his daughter a mother, but Sorcha had lost a sister, a best friend, her *person*. And right when she'd needed Rachel most.

Is that why you berated him in front of the whole bar, including your boss?

Her memories slowed down as she sat up in bed. She hissed at the headache that sprouted behind her eyes and rubbed them to no avail. Gods above, please let the renowned Irish recovery that her father swore by kick in.

She'd never tested the limits of her drinking until the previous night. And it wasn't just the hangover that haunted her.

Oh, God. She had embarrassed herself, hadn't she?

Yep. She owed Mick an apology.

Not Patrick?

Her upbringing said yes, she should make things right with him, too. But her injured heart argued he'd had it coming for a decade and it wasn't her fault he'd waited so long to come back to Boston, on St. Patty's Day no less.

And to think she used to celebrate the holiday.

"Damn," she muttered, padding to the kitchen to remedy the part of her headache that could be fixed with a strong espresso. "Focus on your speech and let the rest work itself out."

She showered and dressed quickly, styling her hair and adding makeup subtle enough that she didn't look as if she was trying too hard, but enough to cover the bags under her eyes. She walked out to the light rail station a block away, tucking her chin against the biting wind that whipped around Faneuil Hall like a wild banshee.

"It's with great pleasure and full understanding of the responsibility that comes with this position that I accept the role of interim chief of surgery," Sorcha said, practicing her acceptance speech.

Thankfully the haze of last night had faded with her last cup of coffee. Perhaps her father was right— the real luck of the Irish was having a banger of a night and being able to bounce back the next day.

For good or bad.

When her sister had gone into the hospital for the very last time, Sorcha's dad had drunk enough each night to float the *Titanic* back to the surface. He'd come in, cursing God in Irish, and Sorcha would wish he'd hurt enough the next day that he'd never want to go back to the bar again.

He had another daughter at home, someone who still needed him.

But he'd wake up almost as if the previous night hadn't happened, leave without a word for the hospital to sit by her sister's side, and then, after a hospital cafeteria dinner, he'd head back to the pub.

It was a cycle of self-pity Sorcha would never repeat. Why not make real change instead?

The light rail arrived and she hopped on, grateful for the lack of people on board. That was usually the case the morning after what was arguably the biggest holiday in Boston.

"I'd like to use this opportunity to keep Dr. Collins's work on track as well as explore clinical trials that can catapult Boston General into the future of surgical interventions."

She didn't need her note cards anymore, but she paused, her mind blank all of a sudden. What came next? Why, suddenly, after weeks of knowing this speech by heart, were the words replaced by an image of Patrick's face, his stony green eyes assessing her, top to toe? His full lips, the bottom one pulled between straight, white teeth while she spilled her dreams at his feet—a distraction already, and she hadn't even started her first day with him.

Sorcha frowned. The city rushed by her at a breakneck speed. In the distance, Fenway Park immortalized the bleeding heart of Boston's sports enthusiasts, bookended by TD Garden, where the Celtics played. The Irish name and colors of the team had always made her feel at home.

"*Ray-chel*'s best friend," Patrick had said. Oh, that *accent. That* was home for her and yet, until she'd heard the rich lilt of his vowels, the way he concentrated on the *r*, she'd almost forgotten where she really came from.

"Trials…" She stumbled on the word. Why was Patrick coming to work at Boston Gen? From what Rachel had said, he couldn't wait to get back to the white sand shores of Bray. "Trials," she whispered. *Oh, yeah!* "Starting with a groundbreaking new surgical technique that will make pediatric neuroblastomas a thing of the past."

The trial that would honor her late sister and

make sure no families went through that kind of loss ever again. What she'd worked her whole life to obtain.

The hospital came into view next, and the lit sign above her announced her stop. She pulled the hood over her head and walked to the entrance of Boston General, as much a home to her as the small apartment she kept.

When the doors hissed open, her future felt like it was doing the same thing. Chairs were set up in the lobby, a stage and podium erected for the announcement of Dr. Collins's temporary replacement, as well as some other important news like the new oncology floor being built in the surgical wing.

Excitement, dormant in her chest cavity since Rachel's death, fluttered to life as if it'd been hit with three hundred volts from an AED.

Until her gaze landed stage right.

Patrick and Mick were shoulder to shoulder, chatting up the president of the board.

Alarms rang in Sorcha's mind.

No, no, no, no, no.

She strode up to the stage and stared at Mick until he finally met her gaze. Guilt lined his eyes.

"Dr. Kelly," he said. She raised her brows in response. "Why don't we talk over here?" He hopped off the stage and led her to the small alcove off the nurses' station.

"Tell me you didn't bring Patrick Quinn here for *my* job, the one I've been working for since I got here, Mick."

He bristled at the use of his nickname. The man was a stickler for the rules—including titles—but had a soft spot for Sorcha. Not soft enough, judging by the way his chin fell to his chest as if in defeat.

"You have to understand, Dr. Kelly. Until last night, I wasn't sure he'd come."

"Yes, but why is he here *at all*?" To her credit, her voice didn't shake near as much as her hands, which she shoved into her blazer pockets. She glanced over and Patrick met her gaze. His expression was neutral, no sense of gloating. Only a mild curiosity.

"I brought him here to help with the new oncology floor."

"In what capacity, Mick?" Forget titles and standing on ceremony. She knew what he was getting at, but wanted to hear him say it.

"He's taking the interim chief position."

"The job you all but promised to me?" she asked. Her voice held only a fraction of the waver she felt. "The one I've worked for, tirelessly day in and day out without so much as a complaint? The one I'm *made* for?"

More like she'd made herself *into* the job trying to get her trial off the ground, but that didn't mean she wasn't a perfect fit.

"Dr. Kelly, we can find something else—"

"I don't want a pity position, Mick. I want the job I earned. No one's worked harder than me, you know that."

He sighed and pinched the bridge of his nose.

Bags under his eyes said he wasn't getting a good night's sleep, either.

"Maybe that should change, Sorcha." She rocked back as if hit by shock paddles. He'd always called her Dr. Kelly. "You do work harder than anyone here, but I have to ask myself why."

She stared at him, willing her chin to stop quivering. "You know why, Mick. You're one of the few people who know."

He put a hand on her shoulder, meant to be comforting most likely. But her skin only itched under the pity and scrutiny.

"What happens if the trial gets rejected? Or better yet, picked up by the Board of Surgeons and taken out of your hands? Then what?"

"Then I get back to surgery," she answered abruptly. But doubt crept in. Rachel had asked her the same thing, what felt like a million years ago. As an impulsive, spontaneous woman, Rachel couldn't ever understand what it was like to work toward one singular goal for any length of time.

This—the trial based on a surgical procedure that would have saved her sister's life twenty years ago if it'd existed—was all Sorcha had.

"Listen. I'm not saying this as your boss. But I'd like to think we're friends after all this time."

"Friends don't sabotage their friends' careers without telling them first," she snapped.

"Fair enough. But I need you to hear this, Sorcha. All I want is your happiness."

"I *am* happy, Mick," she said. But the words sounded flat.

"Find other things to add to your life, Sorcha. Prove to me you're more than this job."

"What's wrong with being dedicated to my career?" she asked. "It's going to save thousands of lives when I get this procedure approved."

"It will. But who will you save next? And when will the tally be enough to give you peace?"

Sorcha rarely cried, not in public or in the privacy of her home. When things were tough, she threw her shoulders back and got to work. Sadness had swallowed her mother whole after Cara died, leaving Sorcha to question why having children was ever worth it. Either way, she'd vowed never to succumb to grief, not more than she could wash away with a night of liquor once a year.

Still, her eyes were damp no matter how hard she willed them to knock it off. One rogue tear fell from her lashes, traitorously landing on her cheek.

Not here, not with him *watching.*

Patrick stood over them on the stage and had likely heard their whole exchange, even though he pretended to fiddle with the sheet of paper in his hands. Fire rose up in her chest, burning away all she'd dedicated her life to. Or rather, handing it over to the man who'd been the cause of so much personal grief in her life already.

"Patrick is here as a favor to me. He's going to use his connections to help the oncology floor go in and we need that now. We'll look into funding your trial when the time comes, okay? But until then, make me this promise, Sorcha. Find joy outside these walls, or trust me—you'll never find peace inside them."

She nodded. What was her other option? To beg for what was rightfully hers in front of the board? In front of the man who'd now robbed her of *everything*?

The doors behind her hissed open again, which didn't grab her attention as much as the way Patrick's eyes lit up, the smile that blossomed on his lips. Objectively speaking, he was as fine a human specimen as she could conjure up in her science-based imagination. Strong, tall, talented. But that smile…

After his terse interaction with Sorcha last night, who knew he was capable of it?

As a woman, she couldn't help but wonder what made him grin like that. She followed his gaze and gasped.

There, in tiny human form with a bushel of red curls and pink frills, was an exact replica of Rachel.

All she had was a name written in the last letter Rachel ever sent her.

"Aoife," she whispered at the same time Patrick shouted to the girl over the crowd. Pronounced like most other Irish words so different from its Irish spelling. *Ee-ffa*. Sorcha had shared with Rachel the name she'd choose for a daughter if she ever had kids, which, given her aversion to familial ties, wasn't likely. So Rachel had "borrowed" the name and asked only for forgiveness.

Sorcha thought she'd prepared for this moment. But she'd miscalculated.

Because nothing could have prepared her for the sweet smile of her best friend's daughter beaming just feet from her as an older woman deposited her in Patrick's arms. Or Patrick laughing with her as he spun her around.

Nothing would be the same after seeing Aoife's wide, happy eyes staring at the hospital with the same awe Sorcha had when she was Aoife's age, right around when Rachel and Sorcha had met, actually.

The walls crumbled, and despite the risk to her heart, Sorcha found herself following her feet toward the girl and her father. The speakers came to life and a man from the board urged folks to take their seats so the meeting could begin. Sorcha ignored him.

Patrick smiled as she approached, welcoming her in.

"Can I meet her?" she asked Patrick.

He nodded. "Rachel wouldn't have had it any other way."

More tears fell, but this time, Sorcha let them. "Hi, Aoife," she said, kneeling on the cold tile floor and offering her best smile, a smile she'd been saving for this moment if it ever came. "I'm Sorcha, your mom's friend from America."

Aoife curled her brow like she was a curious teenager and not the young sprite she was.

"If you're from America, why do you sound like us? 'Cause everyone else sounds funny here. They call me *Oh-iffa* instead of *Ee-ffa* like they're s'posed to."

"Aoife—" Patrick said in a stern tone, but Sorcha waved him off, laughing.

"I know what you mean. For the first few years of school here, people called me 'Scorcher.'"

"You went to school here?" Aoife asked. Her eyes were wide and curious. "I'm going to school soon, to St. Brigid's."

Sorcha nodded, keeping her hands clasped tightly in her lap so she could resist the urge to tuck the girl's wild curls behind her ears.

"It's a good school. And Ireland's only female patron saint."

Aoife nodded. "And she's the one who sends the fairies."

Sorcha's chest constricted. She and Rachel used to ask the fairies for things each night—to watch over friends and family when they were younger, then to turn a boy's head when they became teens, and even now, from time to time, Sorcha would send up a quick ask that the next step of her trial be successful so she could make her impact on the medical world.

"You know, I still ask the fairies for things I need," she admitted. Patrick stiffened next to her.

"You do?" Aoife asked. "I asked my fairies for

things before I left, but I'm afraid they won't find me here."

"Oh, they will. They follow the beat of your heart however far it takes you."

Aoife pumped her fists in the air. "I knew it!"

Sorcha giggled again. "What did you ask them for?"

"I made a list." Aoife tugged on Patrick's sleeve. "Show her my list, Da."

"We should sit," Patrick said, giving Sorcha a glance she couldn't read. It wasn't unfriendly, just…quizzical, as if he couldn't figure her out and wanted to. "They're about to start."

She swallowed hard. "Fine. Aoife, it was nice to meet you. I'm sure I'll see you around."

Especially since your dad is about to be my boss.

"Can we sit by her?" Sorcha heard Aoife ask.

"No, *mo grá*. We shouldn't."

Not *can't*, or *aren't allowed*. But *shouldn't*. What did that mean?

She still cared deeply about the loss from earlier, but she also couldn't stop watching Patrick and Aoife together. They were different than Sorcha imagined. *He* was different. Less…awful, even if he had stolen yet one more thing she cared about.

Oh, Rachel, she thought. *What have you done?*

CHAPTER FOUR

PATRICK MADE IT THROUGH the ceremony announcing not only his new role, but also the hospital's expansion—an expansion he'd oversee. It was work that had the power to change lives.

But he'd barely heard much of the praise accompanying Dr. O'Shea's introduction. His eyes flitted back and forth between his daughter and Sorcha, the former who would wave at him, then Sorcha. The thing was, Sorcha waved back to her, even tossing his daughter a few silly faces.

It was adorable. Or would be, if the woman interacting with Aoife wasn't a complete enigma—and the one variable he hadn't considered when he'd accepted the interim position. And there'd been a lot to consider.

Boston was rife with memories of his life *before*—before Rachel, before his rise to the top of his surgical field, before Aoife. But not many of them were *bad* memories.

He'd seen the Red Sox beat the Yankees after a flyball turned out to be a triple-hitter.

He'd walked the Irish Heritage Trail and marveled at how strong his people were.

He'd stood onstage at graduation as Harvard University's first Irish valedictorian.

He'd met Rachel at an Irish pub just as his residency at Boston Gen came to an end.

However, the secondhand memories that followed, souvenirs of Rachel's fraught trips to visit "home," weren't anywhere near as pleasant. Her parents had taken the news of their elopement about as well as he and Rachel had expected, the weight of her previous spontaneous decisions catching up to her.

Each trip home, their relationship grew worse until, when she got sick, her parents chose not to come to see her. Here she was again, they'd said, following a knee-jerk impulse to carry a baby to term instead of receiving lifesaving medical help.

Patrick sighed. That'd been her last decision, as fate would have it, and the heaviest one for him to carry. He knew what people whispered.

Why couldn't the world-class oncological surgeon save his wife from cancer?

It was a decision he'd replayed at least once a night after Rachel's death—should he have tried harder to push her into treatment? Until he realized something vital, it didn't matter.

He had Aoife, a little ball of love as a gift of Rachel's selflessness. Whether it damned him or not, he didn't think he could make a decision that meant his daughter didn't exist, even if he had the chance.

Look at her, flashing a wink and peace sign at Sorcha.

Ah, Sorcha Kelly.

Rachel's best friend, at least until she'd joined the camp that thought Rachel was making a mistake not getting chemo. What kind of a friend must she be, he'd wondered, if she didn't support her friend's decision and understand how difficult it must've been for her to make?

But... Sorcha wasn't at all how he'd imagined. Rachel had described her as cold and serious and yeah, maybe the night before at the pub he'd seen some of that, but it was understandable, given the circumstances.

The woman currently sticking her tongue out at Aoife didn't seem chilly in the slightest.

Not that he had a clue what to do with that observation. His heart thumped against his rib cage as he observed something else, something far more troubling.

Sorcha was *stunning*, which he hadn't noticed last night, between the sweatpants and fiery words flung in his direction. With her long hair draped across her shoulders, she looked every bit the Irish lass from his homeland, but with curves and strength he'd only dreamed about. To make matters worse, from what he'd gathered late last night as he'd pored over her test protocols on neuroblastomas in youth, she was brilliant to boot.

Too bad, his subconscious argued. *She's so off-*

limits she might as well be the next in line to the British throne.

"Thank you all again for coming," the president of the board said, raucous applause making it hard to hear the soft-spoken man. "Now, let's get to work making Boston General the premier hospital on the east coast."

More applause and then the crowd dissipated.

To his shock, Aoife didn't rush to the stage, even though the nanny he'd hired was on her phone and not watching the girl. He made a mental note to find a replacement as soon as he could. St. Brigid's didn't start for a few weeks yet, and he needed someone he could trust *now*.

His daughter ran to Sorcha's side, hugging her leg. His heart thumped louder than the speakers' whine as the staff disconnected the mic.

Ignore it. You just haven't been with a woman in years.

That had to be why his pulse stayed elevated as if he'd just completed hours of CPR on a patient, not watched his daughter hug a beautiful woman.

He and Aoife were in America for nine months and even if that wasn't the case—if they somehow decided to stay in Boston for longer—his conscience was right. His wife's best friend was off-limits.

She's also your employee.

Aye, she was.

"So, *mo grá*, are you ready to head back with Penny?"

"Do I hafta?"

She stuck out her bottom lip and Patrick almost caved. He should take some time to show Aoife around, but at the same time, Mick needed him to meet with contractors that afternoon to discuss equipment for the oncology floor.

"You do. I'll come home as early as I can, okay?"

She appeared to give that some thought, twisting her lips. Finally she nodded.

"Okay. Only if Sorcha comes to supper," Aoife said. "I want to ask her more about fairies."

Patrick coughed, rocked back on his heels. He threw a glance at Sorcha.

"Um," he said, the words stuck to the back of his throat. "I'm not sure that's a good idea." Not because he didn't want to invite *her* specifically, or that eating with someone other than his daughter was unwelcome. But he and Aoife hadn't had anyone to their home since Rachel passed. He needed... time.

Sorcha's eyes grew wide and her cheeks flushed with color. Ah, Irish skin. It was one of their curses, every emotion flashing across translucent skin like paint-by-numbers art.

"What I mean to say is that we just got here and haven't even unpacked. Let's get settled before we invite houseguests."

Aoife crossed her arms and glared at her father with pouty lips and all.

"Fine. Sorry, Sorcha. My da said no."

Sorcha smiled, and the room brightened. Patrick liked the way her eyes crinkled around the corners.

"Thank you for the offer, Aoife. It was so nice finally meeting you. Your mom was special to me and I like thinking she's watching us now, making sure we get to know each other. Come talk to me anytime you want to hear about her." She glanced up at Patrick. "If that's okay with you?"

Patrick cleared his throat. "Of course. I'll give her to Penny and then get to work."

Sorcha nodded, her mouth open as if she wanted to say something.

"What is it?" he asked as Penny came to take Aoife.

Sorcha worried on her bottom lip.

"I only meant to say welcome to Boston General," she finally said. "You'll be good for the oncological department, and I'm grateful you let me meet Aoife. I meant what I said—Rachel was important to me."

Patrick nodded. "Thanks. And I'm glad you met, too." He'd never seen his daughter take to a stranger like she had to Sorcha. Hell, he'd never been drawn to a stranger like he was to her, either.

"But…" she added, a glint in her green eyes that made her look like her own brand of Irish fairy, albeit one up to no good.

"You know everything you say before 'but' doesn't count, right?"

She only smirked and shrugged.

"But you made me look like a fool last night," she said.

"That was never my intention." He didn't look at the crowd that dissipated into their workstations around the campus, a campus he hadn't even seen yet. "I'm sorry."

"Thank you, but lack of intent doesn't mean lack of impact. You took my best friend, which I'll forgive since that was as much her fault as yours. And now you've taken this job. Dr. Quinn, forgive me, but it's hard to imagine this isn't personal."

"Believe me, Sorcha. Mick never mentioned someone else was vying for the position. Especially not you." Even if he had, would it have changed Patrick's mind? He'd needed the change as much as Mick claimed to need him. It was the only thing that would have inspired him to finally bring Rachel home.

"I wasn't vying for it. I *earned* it after years of dedication to this institution, to the medical advances here. And then you show up and steal it out from under me. Not to mention, Patrick…"

"Yes?"

"You didn't save her when you could have, which I'll never get over."

He stared into her eyes, the passion in them evident.

"Me neither. It's something I'll carry with me to the grave, but if given the chance, I'd never do anything to not have that little girl on this earth, and Rachel felt the same."

Sorcha looked at the doors and Patrick followed her gaze, wondering what she was thinking. This had to be a lot for her to process.

"Anyway, I only mean to say that from now on you owe me honesty."

"I've been honest—"

She held up a hand as if she were, in fact, his chief of surgery. "You didn't tell me why you were here and if we're going to work together, which is impossible to avoid since we're two of the four full-time oncological surgeons. You have to tell me what I need to know to do my job. You owe me that much."

He nodded. How this woman wasn't the boss of everyone he couldn't figure out. He wasn't sure how anyone denied her anything. She was so similar to his daughter. "Deal. If you do one thing for me."

She looked sideways at him. "It depends."

"Tomorrow, I'd like you to show me around where I'll be working. So much has changed since I was here last." Her nod felt like a badge he'd earned. "And start with your research lab. I want to see the medicine you're working on."

CHAPTER FIVE

SORCHA HAD MADE IT THROUGH the rest of the day without seeing Patrick, which meant she could keep her racing heart at least semicalm. He'd asked to see her research, which, given his new title, was his, too. He wielded power over her future, and she didn't like it. Not one bit.

Especially because, the next morning as they walked down the long, narrow hallway, his coconut oil and Irish clover aroma washed over her, bathing her in the scent of her homeland. Wrapped up in a sharp suit that accentuated his masculine physicality, to boot.

She pointed out places of interest to him—the surgical suites, the imaging center, the recovery rooms—explaining that much of it would change as the surgery wing expanded.

It made sense that he'd been asked to head that up. In Rachel's visits, she'd described Patrick's meteoric rise to success in the oncological department at St. Michael's. Cancer treatment needed a certain kind of doctor, one with a precise mind, caring heart, and forward-looking vision.

Was that Patrick?

"What's wrong?" he asked her.

Caught staring up at him, she felt the blood pool in her cheeks.

"Nothing. Sorry. I'm just thinking about the job, honestly. About your vision for the hospital."

His speech at the meeting earlier had laid out his plan to continue patient care without interruption during the build, and how he'd like to grow the department according to Dr. Collins's wishes.

"Do you have an issue with it?"

She shook her head. "No," she admitted. "I'm still processing it. I could have, *would* have loved bringing the patients through the construction myself."

"It would have pulled your focus from the trial at a crucial stage," he said.

"Maybe," she conceded. She couldn't give him the win, even though…he was right. Mick had, in a way, done her a favor giving the job to Patrick. "Except now—"

They'd stopped in front of the opaque glass door with her name across the center.

"Now you wonder how, without the job, you'll get funding for your trial."

She nodded. Turning the corner, they bumped into one another and their hands brushed.

Something sparked where their skin touched, but biologically, she knew that was impossible. It was far more likely that her lack of dating and inter-action with handsome men meant her hormones

and pheromones were fully aware of Patrick's…
attractiveness. Clinically speaking, he was a perfect human specimen.

*That's a classy way of putting it. Admit it—you'd
jump him if given half the chance.*

Maybe that would be true if he wasn't who he
was. If she had an itch, she'd be scratching it somewhere else.

"Um, this is my lab," she said, opening the door.
She was in the lab every minute she wasn't in surgery, but no one ever came back here to check in
on her research. Perhaps that's why Patrick seemed
to fill the space and suck the air from it.

"This is incredible. We didn't have anything like
this when I was here," he said. He ran a finger along
the edge of her stainless-steel table, his eyes glued
to her robotic arm setup.

"You wouldn't have. I built it. Been building it,
actually."

He wheeled around, his eyes wide. "You designed
this? Alone?"

"You don't have to seem so surprised," she
snapped. A sigh followed. "Sorry; this is awkward,
having you here, having to explain myself instead
of focusing on my new position."

The word "my" hung between them.

"I understand."

No "sorry," or, "I'll make it up to you." Just that
he understood.

"Anyway, yes, I did. It's the protocol I told you
about when I—"

When I drank too much and spilled my personal secrets to you last night.

"When I met you."

"Can I see the data?"

Sorcha took a thick binder from next to three others and handed it to him. "This is the set of results from the most recent test, but the preliminary studies are all documented in chronological order in those folders over there."

He gazed behind her and she was struck by the magnitude of the work she'd accomplished when his eyes widened. His fingers tapped the hard plastic of the binder as he scanned page after page. She held her breath in anticipation.

"And you do all this on your own time?"

She bristled, throwing her shoulders back. "I don't waste hospital resources. This comes out of the research budget I received a grant for, a grant that is partially helping to fund the new oncology floor. But the time I spend on it is mine. I still practice and take cases."

Patrick shook his head. *Ugh.* It was the same old story—no one cared about the groundbreaking research if she wasn't actively cutting.

"Listen," she started. "I know you're the boss, but before you got here—"

"Talk me through it," he said. "I want to make sure you have the time you need to pursue this."

Her lips parted and a small gasp escaped her throat. Since he'd been announced as the new interim chief, she'd expected to have to fight against him to gain even a little ground. Yet, here he was, on day two, offering to support her?

"You don't want me to shut it down?"

He chuckled. "That would be shooting myself, and this program, in the foot. But if you already received a grant, why won't that cover the remaining clinical trial?"

She exhaled. "It was money set aside for prelim studies. Next, the results get reassessed by the board and chief of surgery before being allowed to continue. The board earmarks some donor money for expanded trials, and I want this year's allocation. The results speak for themselves."

Patrick's pager buzzed in the sterile silence of the lab. He placed the binder down and checked it, frowning.

"They need us both in pre-op." He strode to the door, then hesitated just before he walked out. "Rachel told me about you, you know. About why this is so important to you."

"The story I told you last night?" Sorcha's skin crawled with awareness. The not-so-gentle reminder this man was inextricably tied to her past was needed.

He nodded, not quite making eye contact with her. "But she told me about your parents, too. I just wanted to say I'm sorry, and I know what this study means to you."

Sorcha willed her pulse to slow.

"It means a lot to hundreds of families who don't know it yet." She didn't know this man near well enough—not even through secondhand stories—to trust him with her truth just yet.

He met her gaze. His was softer than before and the pity—or perhaps kindness?—made her squirm. She'd expected stoicism from the brooding doctor, and that was all she was capable of meeting. Anything more and she'd break.

"We should go," she said, her voice just above a whisper. "If they called us both, it must be necessary."

Patrick nodded and she followed him.

There was pandemonium in the ER. Two sets of EMTs ran in with stretchers heavy with mangled bodies strapped down, each looking worse than the last. Two other pairs of medical transport teams jogged in, blood covering the front of their jackets. The Boston Gen staff called out where to put the patients, while others rushed in and out of rooms. The energy was frenetic and almost feral. Machines and voices blended into a cacophony of sound, jarring after the almost eerie quiet of Sorcha's lab.

"What happened?" she wondered aloud.

He ran a hand through his hair. "Let's find out."

Boston General saw a number of multiple-victim cases a year, either gun violence related, or vehicle crashes. But this seemed different. Sorcha hadn't seen such disfigured bodies before, not outside medical school. Judging by the way the other rooms in the emergency department were being emptied, there must be more victims on the way, too.

Mick waved them over. "Building collapse," he

explained. "Six victims in-house, three obvious head injuries, but they'll all need to be seen for secondary injuries."

"Six more headed here and eighteen being spread out between municipal and county hospitals," Tina, the nurse behind them, shouted as she ran past, IV bag in hand.

"Any news on casualties?" Patrick asked.

"Five so far, probably more by the time the day's done."

"Damn," Patrick muttered. Sorcha nodded her agreement. This was awful—so many lives lost or irrevocably altered from one moment in time. It was the crux of her career, mitigating that where she could, assisting in the healing when she was able. But so much of life was out of her control no matter how well trained she was. "Where do you want me?"

Mick lifted his palms up as if to say, "take your pick."

Tina shouted that she needed doctors and Patrick ran over, Sorcha close behind. Mick came along as well.

"I need two," Tina ordered.

Mick stepped back to let the surgeons in. "Sorry for the short welcome," Mick said. "But thanks for pitching in."

Patrick was already gloved up, assessing the two patients lying side by side. "That's why I'm here."

He took the male patient, who looked like he'd been pulled from the rubble. Gashes across his torso and face were largely superficial, but the thready breath sounds indicated at least one collapsed lung, probably some fractured ribs and other internal damage. But the victims' heads were the real concern. The facial lacerations more than likely meant head trauma.

Sorcha threw on gloves and attended to the patient closest to the door. She pulled out a penlight and assessed brain function. The pupils weren't blown, but there was a sluggishness Sorcha didn't like.

"Call ahead to hold two surgical suites," Sorcha told Tina. She winced. As the interim chief, that was Patrick's call to make. She glanced at him and he nodded his agreement.

"Go ahead, Tina," he echoed. The nurse was new to Boston Gen, but her experience as a trauma nurse in downtown LA meant she came with experience they sorely needed.

Tina hung up the phone. "There's a wait."

"Thanks. We'll have to do what we can down here until something opens." To Patrick, Sorcha called out, "How is your patient looking?" She almost added, "boss," but stopped herself short. It might be true on paper, but he'd have to earn it as far as she was concerned.

"Not great. I'm more worried about the lungs than the head, though. Who do we have that I can call in?"

"Peters is cardiothoracic."

Tina shook her head. "He's not in today. Dr.

O'Shea called him, but he'll be half an hour at least."

Patrick had his stethoscope on the man's chest, a frown on his face. "I don't like it."

"I can assist until Peters comes in. My patient is stable."

"Thanks. We're going to need to perform a thoracostomy and drain some of this fluid if he's going to make it to surgery. Have you done one?"

Sorcha nodded. "I have. What side?"

"Yours. It's clear over here, but the left side is thready."

"Okay," Sorcha said. "Scalpel."

Tina handed her the scalpel and, before she'd even cut, Patrick had the drain tube at the ready. He acted like he'd been on Boston's surgical service for years, not minutes.

She sliced and held out her hand. The tube was there without her needing to say a word. She inserted it, and Patrick had an ear to the patient's chest just as his body convulsed. They turned him on his side, and Patrick kept the stethoscope pressed above the patient's lungs. When his seizure passed, Patrick removed it.

"His breath sounds have improved, but we need to wheel him up *now*. Is your patient stable enough to wait?"

"She'll have to be. That looked like a grand mal."

"I agree. Likely due to the stress his body endured. We've got to find him a room."

Sorcha nodded, placing the tube and hearing immediate improvement. They'd need to perform a back-to-back operation on this patient's heart and lungs if they wanted to save him. But operating rooms had filled up since the accident.

The phone in the ER room rang and Tina answered it. "Surgery one is open," she said.

"Let's go." Patrick hit the button, opening the door, and swung the gurney out. Sorcha followed. If she'd ever believed in the luck of the Irish, she did now.

"We need someone on the female's service," she called to Mick. He nodded and sent another nurse into the room they'd just left. As he'd anticipated, there were three more ambulance teams wheeling victims in. "God, this is horrific. I wonder what building it was."

A nurse ran by with a gauze kit in her hands. "The boutique hotel on seventh. The corner of it is decimated. The news won't stop showing the carnage."

Patrick halted and Sorcha crashed into the gurney. He whipped around to face her, horror on his face.

"Aoife. That's our hotel."

"Go," Sorcha said, her stomach dropping out. "I've got this." He gave her a nod of thanks and sprinted away toward the hospital exit.

Please, please, please.

Sorcha wheeled the gurney to the elevators as

she sent up the same plea she'd asked of the fairies from her childhood.

They may not have listened to her then, but they had to now.

Please let her be okay.

CHAPTER SIX

PATRICK DIDN'T RECALL running the three blocks to the hotel or pushing past the police barricade. He vaguely recalled thanking Penny, then releasing her to her boyfriend who'd driven over to check on her.

The first thing to register was Aoife, still clad in her dress from that morning running into his arms. He held her tight to his heaving chest, choking down sobs as he inhaled her blueberry-scented shampoo.

"Oh, *mo grá*, you gave me a scare there."

"I'm sorry, Da," Aoife said. Her voice was muffled so he released the tight grip he had on her. "It sounded like thunder in the movies. But it's sunny out. Then there were all these sirens."

"Yeah, there was a right bad accident. I'm actually helping some people that were hurt at the hospital."

She pulled back and frowned up at him. "Then why are you here? Don't they need you?"

Patrick's chest ached from the emotion of the last few days—years, even. She'd called him out on his greatest weakness. He'd always choose her. Even at the risk of losing his job, his other family.

His wife.

"I had to make sure you were okay."

His sassy four-year-old put her hands on her hips. "Da, you could have just called, you know."

He laughed then, and tousled her hair, which earned a deep groan of angst.

"I getcha, love. I'm going to have to bring you back with me, okay?"

Aoife smiled, all nods now. "Yes! Does that mean I get to see Sorcha again?"

Sorcha. Damn. He'd left her alone with their patient, who would need two extensive back-to-back surgeries.

"Maybe, but we've got to go quick. Can I carry you?"

"On your shoulders?" She clapped.

"Of course, *mo grá.*"

He was torn square between two worlds—one where he ran off with this child and didn't miss a moment away from her, and another where he got back to work doing what he needed to do to erase the gnawing guilt for letting his wife die under his watch. He might be ready to move on in so many ways, but that didn't mean he'd been absolved of his crimes.

He made his way back to Boston General, his heart rate slowing now that he had the most important thing in his world tight in his arms. The first thing he did was stop at the hospital's day care and ask if they had space.

They didn't, but would accommodate Patrick that week because of the unusual circumstances. He'd have to find an alternative solution between now and Aoife starting at St. Brigid's. They hadn't even moved out of the hotel, though that was changing tonight.

"I love ya, my little gremlin," Patrick said, repeating the phrase he used to say good night to his daughter each evening. "I'll be back soon to check on you, but I've got to see if I can help Sorcha."

"Then go already," she said, shoving him out the door. What was it about Sorcha that had his little girl so intrigued?

Probably the same thing that has you so curious.

He couldn't lie about that. Rachel had had her grievances with her best friend, which he'd understood at the time. But even the limited few interactions with Sorcha had left him feeling like he shared more in common with her than he'd realized.

Before he knew it, he was inside the scrub room, hands sanitized and gloved and being fitted with a surgical mask.

"Where can I help?" he asked as the doors hissed open to the surgical suite.

Sorcha, a trained professional, didn't turn around, but her head tilted up.

"Is Aoife okay?" she asked. "She wasn't hurt?"

Patrick took the assisting surgeon spot across

from Sorcha and for a brief moment, she met his gaze over their masks.

"She's okay." He grabbed a pad of gauze and handed it to her.

She patted the bleeder, from what Patrick could see was a small nick in a vein from the internal damage causing trauma around the patient's good lung.

"Thank goodness. What happened?"

"I didn't stay long enough to find out. But the building collapsed on the opposite side from our room. It's horrific, Sorcha. Debris and mayhem. They won't find all the bodies for days."

"My God." She reached up, and he handed her the number ten scalpel. "Thank you. Wait—you didn't leave her there, did you?"

Patrick shook his head and held the retractor back so Sorcha could fix another bleeder.

"She's here, in day care. For now, anyway."

"You brought her to the *hospital*?" Sorcha asked.

"Where else should I have brought her? We just moved here, and our apartment isn't available until tomorrow."

"Sorry. I didn't mean to talk to you like that. I know you're my boss—"

"I may be your boss, but you can speak freely to me."

She seemed to consider him, passing a brief glance his way. If he didn't know better, he'd say shock widened her eyes.

"It's just a bad time to be here with all the hotel patients... Can you pass me the—"

Patrick already had the suture kit threaded and ready to go. The patient was doing well, all things considered. And thank goodness, too, since they still needed to relieve the pressure in his skull.

"Thank you again." She paused, just before applying the first surgical knot to close the patient's chest. "How do you keep anticipating what I need?"

He shrugged, having wondered that himself. "You're following the same procedure I would."

The steady beeping of the monitor was all that filled the space while Sorcha worked in silence. He assisted where he was needed, the quiet not at all uncomfortable. If he was being honest, he hadn't worked this well with anyone since medical school.

He thought about what she'd said, about him being her boss, and wondered why it didn't feel that way to him. Maybe it was jet lag, or that he was still getting his bearings, but he felt more like they were equal colleagues.

"You said Aoife's in day care *for now*? What did you mean?" she asked, breaking the gentle tension as they both re-gloved and moved to the top of the patient's head. "Take the lead?"

Patrick nodded, and they switched sides without another word. This time it was her anticipating his needs and she handed over a twelve blade.

"Thanks. I need to find something till preschool starts in a few weeks. The nanny I hired from a service is about as observant as a wrong-way driver on a highway. Aoife'll have outsmarted her by the end of the week."

"So," Sorcha said, handing over the bone drill, "what's your plan?"

Patrick waited until the loud whir and crunch of the procedure was over and traded the drill for the gauze Sorcha handed him. Immediately, the pressure in the patient's head dropped. The only thing to do now was to wait overnight before closing him up to see if he was out of the woods and had any deficits.

That, and do the same for the dozen or so other victims in the triage rooms. Patrick sighed as he placed the dressing that would prevent infection, but allow the pressure to continue to drain. It was a simple enough procedure, but any number of complications could occur between now and the next day when they reassessed.

It was going to be a long night.

"I don't have one, to be honest. I'm flying by the seat of my trousers with Aoife. Rachel was... well, she was always the one mothering came easy to. My ma helped out a bunch as well. I love Aoife something fierce, but it's hard to know what to do."

"I don't want to overstep, but would your mom come out to Boston to help?"

Patrick shrugged. "You're not overstepping. I'm... I'm glad we can talk." He was, too. Sorcha's relationship with Rachel was a liability, but also a blessing, it seemed. She understood.

"I don't want to ask her. Coming here was supposed to be for us to say goodbye to Rachel, to fully move on, which we have to do alone. But I'm scared to the marrow of my bones I'm messing it up, you know? That Aoife deserves more than I could ever give her. That it should've been me instead of Rachel."

The gaping silence that followed was heavy and thick. He tried to take a deep breath as he cleaned up, but he couldn't find it. Those last words had lived on his heart for months, years, even, but he'd never let them take flight. Now that he had, he couldn't take them back.

"Sorry. I've never shared that. I apologize if it was too much—"

Sorcha started to walk out. He followed her as the nurses moved the patient into long-term care so they could attend to the next hotel victim. At the scrub sink, she pulled down her mask and met Patrick's gaze head-on.

"When my sister got sick, my dad gave up. On life, sure, but on me, before anything. He wouldn't look at me, didn't do more than drop a plate of take-out in front of me before getting lost in grief. He certainly didn't ever hug me. My mom checked out on everyone for a while, but eventually came back." Sorcha chuckled dryly. "Still, she was so different, so much slower to love and show affection. I know why—that kind of loss sticks to your bones and lungs and makes it hard to function. But I always wished they could be a fraction of the parents you are to Aoife. I can tell how much she loves you and her energy—well, it's because you've made it safe for her to be who she is. That's no small thing."

The deep breath Patrick had been waiting for came in a wave, almost toppling him with the heat that followed. He'd only sobbed openly once before, at Rachel's bedside after she'd given birth to Aoife. As selfish as it was, as much as he'd loved his wife, the moment he'd laid eyes on their little girl, he'd known Rachel had made the right decision to bring Aoife into the world.

Now, he tried to keep the emotion at bay. It wasn't the time, certainly not the place.

"Thank you for saying that," he said, though even he could hear the gruff thickness in his voice.

"And I think I might have a plan to help. Temporarily, at least."

"Wha—" he started, but the rest of the word stuck in his throat. It'd been a whirlwind couple of days. "I mean, why would you help me when I've taken your job and best friend and who knows what else?"

Sorcha smiled up at him. It illuminated the dim, sterile room and broke through the wall erected between them when Patrick had been given Sorcha's position. Maybe there was a way they could get through this without all the awkwardness weighing them down.

"Well, when you put it that way," she teased, before growing serious. "You and Aoife lost so much, too. I don't know you, and I'm not entirely sure I like you just yet, but she deserves to be cared for."

"Okay," Patrick said, his hands on his hips. Curiosity beat out the emotional exhaustion nipping at his heels. "What's *your* plan?"

CHAPTER SEVEN

SORCHA AND PATRICK were a week into her "plan," and all she'd felt since they instituted it was a sharp stab of regret.

Well, that wasn't true. She'd felt *pride* at being able to tweak her research times to care for Aoife while Patrick was still at work on days the hospital day care wasn't able to, until a spot in a preschool opened up. She'd felt *happiness* each time Aoife had run into her arms when Sorcha picked her up from day care, the effusiveness of the child's joy the most contagious thing in the hospital.

The only problem were mental red flags reminding Sorcha that her feelings—joy and self-worth—were fine, acceptable within the range of human emotion, but could spiral out of control into...*love* if she wasn't careful. And love was problematic for so many reasons.

Love led to dependency, which could only lead to loss. She'd seen what it did to her parents when her sister had passed, had felt it in her own way with Rachel's illness, then death.

No, thank you.

Loss was a variable she couldn't control, but love sure was.

Which was where the regret came in. Doting on the four-year-old was fun, especially the parts where Sorcha got to take her out for ice cream, or to the park on a sunny but chilly afternoon. But when Aoife held her hand and squeezed it—half of her wanted to not let go. The other half wanted to run for the hills.

And that was nothing compared to when Patrick met her at the apartment he'd rented for himself and Aoife. What Sorcha felt when he approached her was *much* more dangerous.

He'd been clinical at first, the paragon of professional. The third day, though, he'd smiled at her. The grin had penetrated Sorcha's armor and punched her right in the gut. A gut that was conspicuously warm and squishy every time Patrick was within eyesight. Day six and seven were worse; he'd offered to take them for ice cream, which was fine until he'd paid for Sorcha's and they'd each walked back to the apartment holding one of Aoife's hands.

It was entirely too close to being a family, at least on the outside. Sorcha didn't want another of those, but how could she stop giving that little girl everything she asked for?

How was she supposed to turn off the feelings brewing in her fickle heart for Aoife's father?

It was a mess. Especially since Patrick had asked if he could observe one or two of her patient meetings and surgeries over the next couple weeks—meetings with patients who would be afforded a chance to participate in the blind trial if it was funded.

What was his interest? He either didn't trust her ability to do her job or he wanted to be around her more, and neither was okay. The only thing keeping her tethered to the ground was managing to avoid him at work.

And now he wanted to *purposely* meet? Her heart fluttered.

Knock it off, she admonished it.

"Good morning, Dr. Kelly," Patrick greeted her outside the patient's room. The formality was expected, but it stung a little to lose the "Sorcha" rolling off his Irish tongue in the way her name was meant to be pronounced. Even if it did speed up her pulse each time he said it.

"Good morning, Dr. Quinn."

He smiled, and dammit if it didn't have the same effect on her as her name uttered from his lips. Her stomach flipped and thankfully, she wasn't hooked up to a heart rate monitor.

"Aoife wrote you a letter this morning," he said, his voice lower. He'd also somehow moved closer to her. A problem since she'd had her patient's chart ready to recite and the medical statistics were replaced with the scent of his cologne. Just a hint—nothing overpowering enough to bother a patient. "I'm sorry to say I can't report on its contents since she hid it under her pillow and then tucked it into her jacket pocket this morning."

"She wrote me a letter?"

Patrick shrugged, drawing attention to his broad shoulders draped in a lab coat. He looked both professional, and very much like a movie star playing a doctor on television. Cue her traitorous heart that thumped faster.

He's your boss. He's your boss. He's your—

"Said something about the fairies and how they listened to her ideas."

He brushed it off, but Sorcha's alarm bells went off. Aoife had already confided that she was pretty sure Sorcha had been brought to her by the American fairies. To what design Aoife hadn't said, and Sorcha was in no hurry to unearth that secret. Not if she wanted to keep her distance. "Anyway, it's my tiny terrorist's way of demanding sweets when you're with her. Feel free to tell the girl she can't subsist on ice cream—God knows I've tried and failed on that account."

Sorcha gave a half-hearted laugh and pulled up the patient's chart on her tablet.

"Sorry, Dr. Quinn, but I think we should get this going."

"Sure. Sorry." Why was he apologizing? He was her boss.

About time you *remembered that...*

Sorcha needed to focus on anything other than the doctor who made her feel less like a physician and more like a woman in want of something other than a career. She opened her mouth to rattle off the patient's name, age, diagnosis and prognosis, but stopped.

"Is this observation something you're doing for all the surgeons, or is there something you don't trust about my ability to do my job?"

If that was the case, it meant the feelings she was having—the inappropriate ones—were one-sided. She wasn't sure which way she wanted him to answer.

"No."

Damn. So, he wanted to spend time with her?

He raked his hands down his cheeks and she felt a twitch in her own palms, wondering what the trimmed beard he'd grown out would feel like. In the fluorescent lights of the hallway, it looked dirty blond, but in the daylight, she'd caught hints of red that gleamed.

"I'm sorry if I've been vague. It has nothing to do with your work, Sorcha. Boston General is lucky to have you on its team. I have no reservations about anything you do, honestly. Actually, my interest is in your research, and your patients are a huge part of that."

She opened and shut her mouth twice, unsure of what to say. He hadn't mentioned her research since the day she'd given him a tour of the hospital. A pair of nurses walked by them and giggled to each other after stealing glances at Patrick. He didn't seem to notice them at all, despite their lack of subtlety. Frustration prickled her skin.

"Why?" she finally asked.

"If you're going to apply for the next stage in your clinicals, you'll need a handful of observations and letters documenting how the patients would have benefited from being part of the trial. I'm just getting a head start on that process so when the time comes, you'll be ready. It'll also help the new oncology floor in the surgical wing become established as a specialized cancer center, to have the whole team behind the trial and its implementation."

The initial disappointment that his observation did, indeed, have to do with work gave way to excitement.

"A cancer center?" Her research was so specific, she wasn't sure it was eligible.

"Yes, the American Cancer Society won't list a surgery center on their register that hasn't been through the screening process for at least three clinical trials related to childhood cancers, and yours has three potential different trials that could put it to the front of the line and maybe increase funding possibilities."

"You really did read my research." No one else had ever taken the time, not even Mick. And here Patrick was, a week into the job, not only having read it, but planning her next steps and envisioning broader implications than she'd dared to dream of.

Patrick's brows furrowed and his lips twisted. "Of course I did. It's brilliant, Sorcha. It has a lot of potential, but if I'm being honest, your plan to move forward the application for funding without this kind of scaffolding worries me. It wouldn't have done ya any favors." The slip of a thicker brogue in his speech flicked at her heart, waking it up. "You're onto something but you've got to be patient."

The air around them stilled, charged with a tension now, at least on Sorcha's end.

"Patient?" she echoed. That one word slashed through the recognition of her work, all the kindness he'd bestowed on her. Her racing heart. "I've *been* patient." He swiftly moved them out of the hallway and tucked them into an alcove with patient room supplies. Her limbs tingled with pent-up rage.

"You want me to be patient, do you?" She poked a finger into his chest, but it met with a solid wall of masculine flesh. She winced at the pain shooting up her arm. She felt even more aggravation that *of course* this man was as strong as he was handsome. "That's *all* I've been since I was five years old. Wait for my parents to notice they still had a daughter. Wait to be old enough to go to medical school. Wait for a resident to check off my research. Wait to be allowed to continue what I've worked my whole life on. Wait to get the job that will help me finish this phase of the plan so I can finally start saving children's lives and get back to living my own."

She finished, breathless and hot behind the eyes.

He placed both hands on her upper arms, rubbing them with his thumbs. She hated that it calmed her down.

"You done?" he asked. She nodded, vaguely

aware that she'd poked and screamed at her *boss*. Fire flamed her cheeks. "I didn't mean any harm by saying it, but I won't take it back, either. Your last month of data was rushed, and your funding letter was half-baked at best. If you want to do this, it has to be airtight. You've come too far to let it slip through your fingers because you raced to the finish line without triple-checking each step."

She breathed deeply, filling her lungs with the stale hospital air.

"You're right," she whispered. "I want this. More than anything else in my life, and it was so close to coming to fruition with the interim position. And then maybe, I'd—"

She cut herself off. This man had a way of drawing truths from her as if he was a skilled nurse drawing blood. She barely felt it while it was happening, but this one she caught just in time.

"Maybe you'd what, Sorcha?" Patrick had moved closer, and in the confined space, she felt trapped by his gaze, his scent, his accent. And she wanted all three with the deepest part of her, the part she kept tucked away and out of sight.

Human connection might be a liability, especially when it was combined with intimacy, but in her weakest moments, she craved it on a biological level. Around Patrick, all she seemed to be having were weak moments.

"Nothing. We're running late to see our patient."

"You can trust me, you know. Not because I'm

your boss, or Rachel's husband, but because I want what you want."

Sorcha was thankful for the dim lighting in the small storage space. Maybe Patrick couldn't see the way the heat from her cheeks spread down her neck and shoulders. Because there wasn't any way he wanted what she was too ashamed to admit she desired—him, pressed against her. Hell, she wasn't sure it was actually what she wanted, just that in the moment, it was all she could think about. Guilt at lusting after her best friend's husband threatened to override her senses as much as desire did. Both warred with one another, neither winning out.

Could he sense that, too?

"The study to be funded?" she asked.

He paused, then nodded, stepping back. He put his hands in his pockets and gazed down at her.

"Yes. Of course. The study."

The end of Sorcha's tongue felt tingly as she chewed on Patrick's words. "I… I don't know what to say. Thank you, I guess."

She had been thorough, patient, and focused, which her mom called *tunnel-visioned*, with the data at least. At the risk of having anything resembling a social life. Maybe that's why she was fantasizing about a man who wasn't only her boss, but her dead best friend's husband. There wasn't any other excuse for her inappropriate feelings. She bit her bottom lip as guilt finally won out.

Patrick nodded, his gaze dipping to her mouth.

One hand rubbed his chin thoughtfully. "So, we should get back to the patient, yeah?"

"We should. But thank you for taking an interest." He stopped and his lips parted. She shook her head. She'd never openly desired anyone before—and leave it to her to pick the least okay person as the one her body seemed to want. "In the research, I mean."

"Yes. Yeah. I mean, of course." He walked out of the storage room and through the doorway to her first patient of the day. "So, who are we meeting this morning?" he asked.

Sorcha put on a smile she reserved for her tiny tot patients and followed him into the room, grateful for work that would hopefully distract her from the man just inches to her left. If she couldn't focus and ignore his pull on her, this was going to be an excruciatingly long nine months working with Patrick Quinn.

For her sanity, her research, her future, it was imperative she do just that. Because she'd worked too hard to let her pesky feelings get in the way of her one goal. Except it seemed like it would take an eternity to forget the way her stomach flipped every time she shared a space with Patrick, the way her heart beat as if she'd been jolted by AED paddles when he smiled at her, the way desire for him flooded her nervous system when she let her imagination run wild.

And as he'd just pointed out—she wasn't exactly a patient person.

CHAPTER EIGHT

PATRICK LEFT THE hospital in a daze. The day had been long, with two follow-up surgeries on patients trapped in the hotel. One of them had pulled through and, save some wicked scars, would be able to resume life as usual in a few months. The other victim would never walk again, despite Patrick and his team working a cervical spine miracle to help him keep his legs.

He rubbed his eyes, but they burned with exhaustion. He needed a drink and a twelve-hour nap, but, like the previous five nights since Sorcha's little tirade in the storage room, he was certain sleep would elude him yet again.

It wasn't the work, even though the building renovation coupled with surgeries was mentally and physically draining. In fact, he'd been glad of that so he could go home, make dinner for him and Aoife, then crash when she did.

But that hadn't happened, not once.

Patrick lifted the collar of his coat against the April wind and walked to the elevated train station. Every time he closed his eyes, he pictured Sorcha's cheeks as they warmed with heat, her bottom lip pulled between her teeth, the way her chest—her exquisite chest—rose and fell with each breath. He'd studied the wrong thing in med school, it seemed. Had he known there was an entire woman to dissect, to pull apart each action and word she spoke, he might have focused on a very specific aspect of human anatomy and damn the rest.

But then he'd never have met Rachel... That line of thinking sent the guilt and confusion spiraling from there. His brain went into overdrive the minute his head hit the pillow.

Was a second chance at romance possible after he'd been given a gift as precious as Rachel the first time around, only to squander it?

What would happen if he took Sorcha's hand while they walked down Newbury Street the way his daughter was able to without batting an eyelash? Would her hand be soft and pliable in his?

What would that bottom lip of Sorcha's taste like? God knew that one had kept him up more hours than the rest. Which led to other questions.

He'd loved his wife, but did his new feelings for Sorcha negate that? *Possibly.*

Did he feel lecherous lusting after a surgeon under his care? *Absolutely.*

Were Sorcha's own feelings about Rachel too complex to even consider blending them with his own? *Likely so.*

Was he capable of letting all of this go and getting to sleep so he could function at the top of his game? *Definitely not.*

The train came and Patrick stepped inside, the warm air like a balm to his heart. Unfortunately, it also made his eyelids that much heavier.

The whole thing was a mess, especially since he still had to find the courage to reach out to Rachel's parents, to introduce them to their granddaughter and say a final goodbye to his wife. It was getting harder and harder to do that, the longer he spent with Sorcha. What if they saw right through him for even considering another woman while his wife's ashes were still in his possession?

He walked up the stairs to his building and sighed.

That's not what's happening. I'm allowed to move on at some point. I have to, for Aoife's sake. I still love Rachel. I always will.

Not that it mattered. It wasn't like Sorcha had ever shown him anything other than mild professional courtesy; any actual kindness was aimed toward his daughter.

So, why couldn't he stop thinking about her as *more*—so much more—than just a colleague?

He took a deep breath and put his keys in the lock, opening the door to his and Aoife's apartment. Just thinking about his wife and Sorcha in the same breath sent waves of guilt crashing against his chest, where memories of life with Rachel lived.

A shriek greeted him, followed by another, louder, high-pitched squeal. They acted like a jolt of caffeine jabbed straight in his heart. He tore off to the back room where the sound came from, and stopped short when he turned the corner.

Oh, thank the gods.

He sighed with relief at the sight of Aoife doubled over laughing. He leaned an elbow against the door frame and took deep, calming breaths. She was okay, so he was, too. Until he glanced over at Sorcha on the floor, her red hair spread out like a crown of fire. Her shirt was inched up just above the waist of her jeans, giving him a peek at her taut stomach.

Oh, no. That small swathe of perfect, creamy skin was sure to take a starring role in his nocturnal imagination that night.

She giggled, her cheeks a different sort of red than they'd been around him. Her eyes were brighter, too. Till they landed on him. She sat up and ran her fingers through her hair, making his own fingers twitch with jealousy. Her light green eyes grew into jade stones.

"Patrick," she whispered, standing up and tugging down her shirt. She held his gaze and a fire grew in his chest. *This.* This was what confused things—the appearance of what a family might look like with Sorcha as part of it. Each time he had that thought, his memories of Rachel faded ever so slightly.

"Da!" Aoife yelled, and catapulted into his arms. He hugged her tightly, but his eyes didn't leave Sorcha. She'd pulled that infernal bottom lip between her teeth again. Couldn't she see it unraveled his good sense each time she did that?

"Looks like you've been having fun," he said to his daughter. He put her down on the floor in front of him and realized from her luminous smile how true the statement was.

"Oh, the absolute best! Sorcha and I were writing notes to the fairies and letting them know I still need a puppy—"

"Which I explained can't happen since Irish fairies can't risk the puppy falling into the Atlantic Ocean on their trip over. She'll just have to wait until she's home to have one," Sorcha added.

He mouthed, *thank you*, over Aoife's head. Sorcha nodded. But his heart thumped a little harder when she said "home." For the first time since he'd left for American medical school, he didn't picture "home" as his flat in Dublin. Hell, the image of Ireland didn't crop up at all.

Unfortunately, what did was a lot like this, Sorcha included. He swallowed hard.

"I know…" Aoife crooned. "But I had to put something in this letter. 'Specially since the fairies already brought me you, Sorcha."

The red painted on Sorcha's cheeks deepened, and he wondered if there was heat behind the color as well.

"Aw, that's sweet. What was it you asked the fairies for?"

Aoife nodded, running to her wardrobe. She retrieved the crinkled piece of paper Patrick recognized, and he froze as Aoife pointed out the bottom item on her list. His throat constricted and he held his breath, waiting to see Sorcha's response instead of intervening to change the subject.

Her chest hitched and her eyes welled with moisture. Was that the quirk of a smile playing on her lips, or was he imagining what he wanted to be true?

No, you don't want her to want you that way. She was Rachel's best friend, and you stole her job. Those feelings are bound to confuse things.

He ignored his overbearing conscience.

You still have Rachel's ashes on your mantel.

He accepted that particular admonition, but still, his heart saw things a little differently. How could it not, when this woman was so magnificent with his daughter?

That's not entirely true, either. His conscience jumped in again. *You respect her for how she treats Aoife, but you like her for other reasons.*

That was closer to the truth, wasn't it?

Sorcha was good craic, and knew how to have a laugh.

She was brilliant at her job.

She cared for people more than they'd ever know...

Was *he* one of those people?

"You asked the fairies for a new mother?" Sorcha asked. She glanced up at him, her eyes searching his.

"I did. My da said the only thing less likely was

a puppy, so do you think, now that I've found you, I could get one of those spotted dogs like the one in the park yesterday?"

"Oh, darling, that's a Harlequin Great Dane. They're more horse than puppy. Let's think through some other options that wouldn't give your *da* a heart attack. Now, why don't we clean up this mess so the fairies are more inclined to grant you two days of ice cream in a row."

Sorcha smiled and patted Aoife on the head, changing the subject for him. What did she think about Aoife's proclamation, though? She'd made it pretty clear she'd had a rough upbringing but did she want a family of her own? Maybe he'd ask her that evening—just out of curiosity, of course.

Hopefully her answer would provide some needed clarity to his other questions.

He looked up images of the Great Dane they must've seen. Sorcha was right—they were half equine to be sure. But they were beautiful. Graceful despite their size. And the black-and-white-spotted puppies… They were hilarious, floppy things. He chuckled, then stopped himself when the ladies looked his way. Something about the way Sorcha smiled at him loosened the knots in his throat.

He clicked out of the search. Who would watch the puppy while he was in surgery? Would they bring the small pony back to Ireland? No, obviously not.

Clearly he wasn't in the right state of mind to think through major decisions when he was this exhausted and hungry. Best let everything percolate and then dive in when his head was clearer.

"Where are we eating tonight, girls? I don't think I can do another lobster roll."

"Now you hush before the food gods smite you where you stand. Lobster rolls are heaven," Sorcha said. She scooched past him to put some books on the shelf, and he caught a whiff of spun sugar with some kind of floral undertones. Lilac, maybe?

He inhaled it into his lungs. Hell, the woman had infected him skin, mind, and heart, and she didn't have a clue. What would she think if she could read his sordid mind, the thoughts he had of kissing her and seeing if she tasted as good as she smelled?

She'd smack him back across the Atlantic was what she'd do.

"I like them, too, Da," Aoife said, hands on her hips and bottom lip pouted just so.

He sighed. Was there anything he'd deny her? His gaze flitted to Sorcha. Aoife thought she wanted another mother, but what would happen if Patrick entertained that? Would she grow up and feel betrayed that he'd moved on so quickly?

"Okay, then which food truck? MacMillan's or Finn's?" he asked. Anything to give his mind and heart some rest from the relentless pelting of questions he had no answers to.

They cheered and he had a startling thought.

He didn't know much, but he'd eat lobster every meal for the rest of his days if he could keep those smiles on their faces.

* * *

The alarm echoed off the vaulted ceiling in the bedroom. Patrick yawned and rubbed the lingering sleep from his eyes before stretching. Man, was he tired, all the way to his bones and the marrow inside them.

He'd gotten a better night's sleep than he'd had in over a week, but his dreams were strange and filled with scenes that left him wary and unsure where he was when he awoke.

For starters, when the alarm had first startled him awake, his hand had reached over and patted the still-made side of his bed. What had he been looking for?

He sat up and frowned.

Oh, yes. In his dream, Sorcha had been tangled in the sheets with him, her lips on—well, on places that made him half-hard just imagining it for a fraction of a second. He let the rest of the dream evaporate, but its aftereffects lingered while he dressed, dropped Aoife off at the hospital day care and walked to his office.

He might've gotten more sleep, but he sure as hell wasn't more rested.

On the way, he checked his email.

"Holy hell," he whispered when he saw one from the board, copied to Mick.

The subject line simply said: Re: Kelly Neuroblastoma Clinical Trial—APPROVED.

"She did it."

He didn't have time to process the good news,

however. Mick caught up to him, two paper cups of what had better be straight espresso.

"Hey, there, Chief. How's it going?" Mick asked, handing Patrick a coffee.

"Pretty damn good, actually."

"Really? You look exhausted."

"Thanks," Patrick said, throwing back the scorching coffee and dumping the empty cup in the trash. He didn't even care that his taste buds were torched. The pain woke him up more than the caffeine would. "You get the email?"

"I did. Good news for Sorcha."

"For the hospital, too. That why you're following me to my office?"

"No, actually."

"Well, then, to what do I owe the honor?"

"I can't just want to talk to my good friend and find out how he's warming to being back in Boston?"

Patrick glanced at Mick whose eyes were downcast. "I've got some news I can't wait to share with someone much cuter than you. I've no time to chat," he teased.

Mick sighed. "I want to check on Sorcha. I haven't been able to connect with her lately, and I'm concerned about how she's taking things."

"What do you mean?"

Mick shrugged. "She's not in her lab when I swing by, and she's *always* in her lab. Hell, I had to lecture her about taking a break now and then.

I'm worried she's depressed or something. Have you seen her?"

Patrick swallowed hard, his mind trailing back to the end of his dream that morning.

Not the way certain parts of my anatomy would like to.

"She's fine, far as I can tell. Been helping me out with Aoife."

Mick's mouth fell open. "She's *babysitting* for you?"

"I wouldn't call it that," Patrick said, annoyance creeping into his voice. Technically, Mick wasn't wrong, but it felt different somehow. Like they were a family of sorts. An unconventional family, but a caring, functional one nonetheless.

"Call it what you want—she's spending time with your daughter instead of working on her research? Does she know the trial has been approved?"

"No. I haven't seen her yet. But I'll let her know as soon as I do. Don't worry—she's up to the task of taking it on. Aoife and I won't get in the way." Why had Patrick added himself to the mix?

"Did you bribe her? Perhaps blackmail her with some sordid secret from her past?" Mick asked, still incredulous. Patrick frowned and crossed his arms. Mick threw up a hand. "Fine, fine. I'm not concerned about her work ethic, don't worry. I've just never seen the woman take more than a day off from the lab, and that was for a conference on pediatric neuroblastomas. I'm surprised, is all."

"It was her idea. Now, anything else I can help

you with or can I get back to work making your hospital fabulous?"

Mick had the audacity to grin, hinting at a joke Patrick wasn't in on. "Sorry to bug you. Carry on and keep…doing exactly what you're doing."

Patrick's frown deepened, as did his confusion. "I will." He shook his head as Mick sauntered off, looking awfully pleased with himself.

Jeez. I need an IV of coffee and five minutes with my thoughts so I can plan out the trial's announcement to the public without Sorcha's scent infecting my rational thought and my boss being cryptic. And I have to find her to share the good news. Maybe then she'll forgive me for taking her job.

Patrick rounded the corner and stopped. Okay, maybe he'd get two of those accomplished right away. Never mind that they were out of order.

Sorcha was there, pacing outside his office. His heart palpitated in his chest.

"You're here early!" he proclaimed as he walked up. He smiled, unable to stop that little tic whenever he saw her. She didn't return more than a furrowed brow.

"I got called in by a nurse at the request of a family."

"They couldn't wait until you got in at seven? I'll talk to them—"

She put a hand on his arm and shook her head.

"What's wrong?"

"I know the family. Their little girl has been in twice before and this time…this time it's bad. I need your help," Sorcha said. He nodded, already willing to give her whatever it was she wanted.

"Anything."

"I can't quite figure out an approach for this patient." The frustration showed on her face and in her voice. He'd bet she wasn't stumped all too often.

"Show me the X-rays?"

She nodded. "They're up in the lab."

Seconds later, he stood in front of X-rays that were bleak at best. Sorcha had undersold the twisted neuroblastoma that greedily took up a large portion of the patient's films.

"Oh, no," he whispered, reaching for the chart on the desk in front of the images.

"She's seven, this is her second tumor," she said as he read the same information. He closed his eyes. A parent's worst nightmare. No wonder the hospital had called Sorcha in. Her bedside manner and surgical brilliance made her a favorite among the surgical staff. "The first one we resected, but this time, it's twisted around her spine."

Patrick pinched the bridge of his nose. "She'd be a candidate, wouldn't she?" he asked.

"If the trial was fully funded and ready to go, she would."

Which it wasn't. He was itching to tell her the good news, but it wouldn't help this patient, so he kept the celebration close to his chest. Best to keep her focused so Sorcha could save this little girl now. So they *both* could—this surgery would take two

accomplished surgeons, and even then he wasn't
sure they could pull it off.

"What do you want to do?" he asked.

Sorcha leaned in toward the X-rays and ran a
finger along the border of the white strand of the
tumor.

"I want you to help me find a way to save her."

Patrick inhaled and let the air calm his tachy-
cardic heart. He didn't know if it was possible, especially since the trial wasn't going to be up and
running soon enough. They weren't even meeting
about the trial until the beginning of next month,
and this patient didn't have that long. Bureaucracy
would kill more patients than tumors.

Damn if he wasn't going to do everything he
could, though—for the patient, sure. But also for
the woman standing next to him.

After they saved the young patient's life, he'd tell
her the news that would change both their lives and
the lives of thousands of patients.

He smiled, despite the tension in the imaging
room.

"Okay, let's make a treatment plan. And then, I'd
like to grab a coffee and talk."

CHAPTER NINE

SORCHA WORRIED ON her bottom lip while Patrick scribbled on a tablet. She had her own open to the latest literature on neuroblastomas and spinal implications, but it didn't matter. This was the third time she'd read it that morning.

"We could go in through the front," she offered.

He nodded, but his frown said that wasn't the best approach.

"Or we could start with a posterior attack, get what we can, and then use chemo and radiation to shrink the rest."

"Maybe." Patrick opened his mouth to say something else, then frowned and closed it again. When he repeated the action twice more, Sorcha clicked off her tablet.

"Is it really hopeless?" she asked. The "without my clinical trial being funded five weeks ago" was implied.

"No. But you're not going to like what I'm thinking."

He turned the tablet toward her. The patient's scans were marked up with yellow and red highlighter, making the tumor look like part of a video game racecourse instead of a death sentence for a child not even old enough to play video games.

"You're right. I don't like it. Not one damn bit."

He scribbled something illegible in the corner. It wasn't the time to notice, but Patrick was adorable when his lips were twisted in concentration. What would it take for him to soften them, to relax?

"We can—"

She held up her hand. "I don't like it, but we don't have a choice. I agree with you that this is the best course."

"Are you sure?" he asked.

She nodded, and this close, his scent—that damned coconut oil and Irish pine—snuck around her throat, choking it like an invisible tumor that was less deadly, but still its own brand of dangerous.

"Okay. Let's get prepped, but I'd like to use your posterior approach if we get in there and it looks different than the scans show. This tumor's a beast, and I wouldn't put it past the thing to have grown since we took the images."

"I wish the trial was able to help her," she said quietly.

Patrick's face twisted. "I'd like to talk to you about that, but let's help your patient first," he said.

"It's your plan, so she's your patient. I'm just assisting on this one." Even though that was true, Sorcha mentally added Elsie to the growing list of patients that needed her trial. Even if it were approved today, it wouldn't be far enough along to change the need for this surgery, but the other patients like Elsie out there waiting…

Patrick was right; she had to go step by step or risk losing it—and every patient it could help. The thing was, it'd been easier of late to be more patient, to concentrate on something other than just her research.

Spending time with Aoife was hardly an imposition. In fact, it was nice to appreciate human interaction, and feel joy, again.

And then there was Aoife's father. Sorcha didn't mind the days and evenings in Patrick's presence as much as she had in the beginning. This man was so much more than a person who'd stolen her job, abandoned her best friend. She wasn't sure he'd actually done either. He was a man who'd woken her up to all she'd forsaken in the name of research, but how could she let those feelings take root when her other feelings—about caring for Rachel's husband and daughter—were the actual complication? Even if she looked forward to Patrick coming home at the end of the day, what could she really do about that?

Home.

It was *his* home, not hers; good grief, she had to stop imagining that he felt the same deep desire she did. But the sight of his smile when he walked in the door, his pronouncement that he'd be taking them to dinner before walking Sorcha home—she'd be lying if she thought her good sense had stuck around past meeting Patrick that first day.

Oh, Rachel. I'm so sorry.

Sorcha wasn't entirely sure what the apology was for, but she felt it reverberate in her bones.

She sighed and focused on the scans in front of her. This was what mattered most, or at least it should. Yet, somehow, against all reason, Sorcha found herself wanting more. Was that possible? She didn't know, but now wasn't the time for her to try to figure out her personal life. She had work to do.

They had work to do.

She didn't want to think about a young life cut short. If she did, she'd be forced to reckon with her own story that was marred by the same loss.

"Let's give this little girl her life back," she said.

Six hours later, the room erupted into applause as Sorcha put her tools back on the surgical tray. She grinned like a kid at Christmas behind her mask. They'd traded off midway, her approach the better one after all.

As a team, they'd done it; they'd saved Elsie.

"Congratulations," Patrick said, his eyes gleaming behind the protective glasses they wore. "You were incredible."

"We all were. Thanks, team." She turned to Patrick as she handed over the patient to the nurse to bandage.

She and Patrick stripped off their gloves and pushed through the heavy doors to the sterile washroom adjacent to the operating room. She pulled down her mask and inhaled deeply. Only now did she let the nerves from before seep through. Her fingers were still steady—years of practice ensured that—but her bottom lip quivered.

"Thank you for trusting me with a plan B instead of scrapping the surgery."

Not many surgeons she knew would have relinquished control and admitted her plan was better.

"Of course. Pivoting is vital if it means we can save the patient." Patrick washed his hands and watched her closely. "How are you?"

"Good," she lied. "I mean, it was an interesting case." She glanced through the window, at the small figure on the operating table.

"How old was your sister when she was diagnosed?" Patrick asked. How he understood so much without her saying anything astounded her. She'd known him for such a small length of time.

"Three. But she passed at seven."

Heat built behind her eyes, but she forced it back. This was neither the time nor place to stroll down that particular memory lane. Most of the time, the loss sat squarely against her heart, quiet and ever present, but her muscle was growing around it. It was mostly a driving force now, propelling Sorcha toward her singular goal—fund the trial and let it save countless children who would be luckier than her sister.

Which, if the board agreed, she'd get the opportunity to do.

"All we've done is buy her time. She'll need more than what we did for her today if she wants to go to her first school dance, to fall in love, or to find a fulfilling career. She needs—"

"To be part of your clinical trial," he said.

Sorcha nodded.

Patrick's eyes were trained on the young girl on the operating table, and Sorcha wondered if he was picturing Aoife there. It was a parent's worst nightmare, seeing your child go through something like that and being powerless to help.

Except he could. They both could.

When he turned around and faced her square on, she almost reeled at the intensity of his gaze. His eyes were emerald molten lava, liquid and emanating heat. He put a hand on her arm and his skin branded hers.

"Sorcha, you got it."

"Got what?" she asked. His smile was so out of place and yet familiar.

"The funding and approval from the board." He *couldn't* mean the trial funding because she hadn't submitted her paperwork yet… His smile deepened. "For your trial."

He squeezed her arm affectionately and maybe it was the human contact, or the fact that she finally understood what he was saying, but a few rogue tears escaped.

"But…*how*?" She wiped at her cheeks, which were damp. "When you got the interim position, I—" She choked out a sob when she realized what she'd done; she'd all but abandoned her work, partly out of grief, and partly out of appreciation for something new in her life.

A connection with two people who were growing to mean something to Sorcha, despite her adamant fear about letting anyone in.

"I never sent the final paperwork to the board."

He leaned in and whispered, "I did. After your final tweaks, it was ready to go and just needed chief approval."

"Okay. I mean, wow." Her trial was approved, *funded*, and she would finally be able to save lives. But...

"You didn't tell me you did that."

"I know, but I wanted to make right what I took from you."

It was a sweet gesture, but the circumstances... It was too reminiscent of her childhood where every decision was made for her, where she'd had no agency, no voice.

"Thank you. But can you promise me something? Include me in anything that concerns me next time, please."

He frowned, as if he hadn't even considered how his gesture could have rubbed her the wrong way. "Of course. Sorry."

"It's fine," she said. "I just deserve to know where we're at with something I've worked my whole career on." Still, excitement fluttered in her chest.

"Agreed. And I'm sorry. Set a meeting with me next week. We'll make a plan for what the trial will do to your caseload. But I have one stipulation."

"What's that?" There was always something. At this point, she'd all but sold her soul, her family, and her future for this, so what was one more concession?

"Let me work on it with you. You'll need other surgeons willing to help you on this project. I want in, Sorcha."

He took a step toward her, his gaze intense and unflinching. Between the musical quality of his accent and the way his green eyes resembled the hills of southern Ireland in the sunlight, she felt her own brand of powerlessness around Patrick. She all but forgot about her frustration with him.

Sorcha's heart rate increased.

"Why are you doing this?" she whispered. "If it's pity—"

He shook his head, cutting her off.

"I assure you it's not. Your study is what's funding my ability to be here with Aoife, to say goodbye to Rachel." Sorcha winced at the mention of her best friend. Would they ever be able to talk about her without guilt and shame tainting the conversation? "I don't take that lightly. Besides, I've seen the science. What you're proposing works, and I'd like to be part of bringing it to life."

Sorcha couldn't stop the rest of the tears from falling to her cheeks.

"Thank you, Patrick." She put a hand on his, no longer able to ignore the pulse of energy that sang along her skin where they touched. He leaned in, dipping his chin.

Is he going to kiss me?

God, she wanted him to, wanted to know what he tasted like, and what his hands felt like tangled in her hair. She was surprised by the pulsing need thrumming beneath her rib cage.

But—

She forced herself to picture Rachel's smile, the one in the picture she'd sent Sorcha after her elopement to Patrick. When that didn't work, Sorcha reminded herself about her no-strings-no-hurt mantra.

But what if...what if we just spent the night together? Would that really be so bad? Is he a man you can spend one night with and call it good? What about his daughter? The fact he was once Rachel's husband? Could you ignore all those things?

As he leaned closer, only the scent of hospital soap and something so wonderfully masculine separating their bodies, she thought she might like to find out.

She didn't get the chance. The door opened and the nurse walked in, thankfully chatting with the anesthesiologist behind her so she didn't seem to notice the tension filling the small space.

Patrick cleared his throat and stepped back.

"Congratulations, Dr. Kelly. I'll see you first thing next week in my office."

With that, he walked out of the room, leaving her with the rest of the surgical team. His absence left a vacuum of desire in its wake but also the ability to think without being overwhelmed with the presence of a man who was changing her biology, making her want the unattainable.

But the same man had just delivered the dream she'd spent her whole life chasing.

"Woot!" Sorcha exclaimed the minute the doors shut behind him. The nurse and anesthesiologist startled. "Sorry, just excited."

"It was a good surgery. Congratulations, Dr. Kelly."

It was a damn fine surgery, but with her clinical trial approved, risky surgeries like the one she and Patrick had just performed were going to become increasingly rare. As long as Patrick kept his word, the trial was a go.

She did a little dance, her hips swaying in her scrubs, the mask around her neck joining the party. She almost forgot the way Patrick's eyes had glittered when he was mere inches from her, the way her stomach flipped with recognition at the way he looked at her, the suspicion he wanted her the same way she did him.

Ignoring his pull on her, she concentrated on the pervasive thought she'd been waiting to voice her whole life.

"We did it, Cara," she whispered victoriously. "We finally freaking did it."

CHAPTER TEN

PATRICK SLAMMED OPEN the door to his office. The hinges creaked under the force and the lab door next to him opened. A timid head peeked out.

"Sorry. Door just caught the wind."

The brunette with pink tips frowned and shut her door again.

Patrick sighed and pinched the bridge of his nose once his own door was shut carefully—and quietly—behind him.

What were you thinking? he chastised himself. *You almost kissed her in the middle of the scrub room.*

His fingertips still tingled where they'd grazed her arm. He ran them through his hair instead.

Honestly, what *had* he been thinking? That Sorcha would be so moved by his ability to do his job that she'd want to find the nearest supply closet and leap on him? What a fool he was.

The damned thing of it was, though, he got the overwhelming sense she was meeting him halfway.

It didn't matter if she'd jumped in his lap and

said, "Do me, Doctor." Sorcha Kelly was hands-off, thoughts-off—forbidden in every sense of the word.

To start with, he couldn't think of her without thinking of Rachel—hardly a recipe for moving on. And what about Aoife? Sure, Sorcha and his daughter got along, but Aoife was too young to know how this might affect her future.

There was also the fact that he and Aoife were only in Boston for several more months. It'd seemed an eternity on the flight over; if he'd believed in fairies like Aoife, he'd have asked them to help him blink and it all be over, back in his own bed with his goodbyes to Rachel behind them.

But now…

Now he wanted someone else—a colleague, no less—and with each day that passed, he wanted less and less for the time to pass quickly. What a curse it all was—to desire something so far out of one's reach and want it more than anything else.

One last, insurmountable thing stood in his way. Though it was a small physical object taking up no more room than a flower vase on his mantle, it loomed large, blocking his view of anything beyond it.

It was time to say goodbye to Rachel—not her memory, which would always linger, but to his past. Maybe then he'd have an idea what to do with his future.

Patrick dialed a number he'd memorized but never used. It rang twice before a man's gruff voice answered.

"Hello?"

"Good evening, Mr. Walker." Patrick ran damp hands down his slacks. It was stifling in his office. He waited, silence the only thing greeting him on the other end. "It's Patrick Quinn."

"I know who you are. Figured I'd get this call a couple months ago when you first got here."

Patrick squeezed his eyes shut. If he wasn't a coward, he would have. He'd feared that looking into Rachel's father's eyes, seeing the grief he blamed on Patrick, might undo all the work Patrick had done to try and move on.

"I'm sorry it took so long. But I brought Rachel home to ya. And our daughter, Aoife." *There*. He'd said it, he'd opened the gates.

A deep sigh reverberated through the line, laced with years of disappointment.

"You'd better give me time to break the news to Joanna. You can come by tomorrow afternoon, both of you. I can't promise much, but we'll be there to greet you. I'll text you the address."

Patrick agreed and hung up the phone. His hands trembled, not a brilliant thing for a surgeon.

He strode out of his office, his brain temporarily on hiatus after almost kissing his coworker and calling his former in-laws. He wasn't sure where he was heading, just that his body needed to move.

Aside from the impossible—saving Rachel's life through some magical, nonmedical means—he wouldn't have done anything differently. Aoife was a light in all his dark places, dark places that had existed while Rachel was alive. Any circumstance that led to Aoife not existing wasn't one he'd consider rewriting.

That had once led to crippling guilt, but it had lessened with time, until the only remorse remaining was his lack of guilt altogether.

Now, faced with a date and time to face Rachel's parents, it crept back.

Patrick passed by the surgical suites, noting the progress with the build. It was a slow process, but Patrick's meetings had been fruitful, and it looked like the board had approved funding for the upgrades to the equipment he'd suggested. There wasn't any use in having a new lifesaving space with out-of-date tools.

Speaking of lifesaving… Patrick realized he'd stopped in front of Sorcha's lab.

He ran a hand along the name placard on the door.

Dr. Sorcha Kelly

How many times had he heard that name, wondered about Rachel's serious supposed best friend who'd never made it to the Irish shores where Rachel lived? His wife had spoken about Sorcha first with awe, then with her own grief attached. In the last weeks of her life, she'd opened up about how her impulsivity had ruined nearly every relationship she'd ever had, including those with her parents and Sorcha.

Whenever he and Sorcha talked about Rachel, the hurt was mirrored in her bejeweled eyes. Once this meeting with Rachel's parents was over, maybe he and Sorcha could talk about Rachel, too. Not with judgment, but a sense of shared history.

The door swung open and a shocked Sorcha stood there, staring up at him. Her gaze dipped briefly to his lips, then a flash of pink painted her cheeks.

It undid a knot in his stomach, which had the simultaneous effect of sending blood to a part of his anatomy that wasn't invited to this conversation.

"Patrick." She shook her head. "Sorry, I mean Dr. Quinn. What are you doing here? Is Elsie okay?"

He cleared his throat. "She's fine. I'm just…walking around. Checking on the build. And you?"

Could she see the lie written on his face? Because what had actually happened was him following a magnetic urge to her door.

She licked her bottom lip and he swallowed a groan. What was it about her that had him reacting like a horny teenager instead of a medical professional who could separate a hormonal response to a beautiful woman from a bad decision?

"I'm headed to the cafeteria to eat a quick dinner before I dive into this next set of research. How is it coming along? The build, I mean."

He shrugged, more interested in her research— and also how her lips stayed that perfect shade of pink without lipstick.

"Good, I think. Do you mind if I join you? I'm starving."

She shut the door behind her and her lab coat got

stuck. Frustrated, she opened the door again, freeing herself. Patrick swallowed a chuckle. Sorcha wasn't at all what he'd pictured. Yes, she was easily frustrated, but behind that was an intellect that was inspiring. Instead of the hard, overly focused woman Rachel imagined her friend to be, Patrick saw a flexible, dedicated doctor and friend.

Friend?

For now…

He'd stopped denying he wanted more and focused on figuring out why and how she'd broken through his iron-clad gates.

"Sure." She stalked down the hall at her usual breakneck speed, but his long strides easily kept pace. It was adorable that the woman seemed to go everywhere with purpose. "What about Aoife? Don't you need to get home to her?"

"I do, and I will. But I hired one of the hospital day care employees as a sitter so I could get some work done tonight. I've got a couple hours left."

"Why do you only *think* things are going well with the build?" she asked, slowing halfway down the hallway to gaze up at him. He nudged her right at the fork instead of left to the cafeteria. "Wait, where are we going?"

"A secret dinner spot I discovered. Is that okay?" She nodded and he tucked her crooked smile into his memory for later, along with the catalog of her other idiosyncrasies.

They got to a side door of the hospital and he pushed it open, fighting against the wind. Sorcha tightened her coat around her core, shivering. Patrick took off his overcoat and wrapped it around her shoulders. The look she gave him with bright eyes that reflected the clouds above was a mix of appreciation and curiosity.

"Thank you," she whispered.

"No bother. Anyway, to answer your question, some shifts need to be made if we're going to make real progress in opening up access to the new floor. It's why I'm so glad your trial was approved."

"What do you mean?" Sorcha tripped, not exactly out of character, but it warmed him to his core that he was there to catch her. He left his hand on the small of her back, which all but made the chilly Boston air impermeable. He could have heated the whole city.

"Your trial doesn't care about employer insurance or premiums. It's just…good medicine." The way she beamed up at him, like he'd discovered vaccines himself, made him want to be a better man, better father, better doctor. He coughed. "So, where in Ireland is your family from?"

"Dingle," she replied.

"A west coaster, eh?" He tucked her tighter into him, and he marveled at how compactly she fit into the nook of his shoulder and side, as if he was made to support her. "I thought I detected a hint of a Kerry accent."

She playfully jabbed him with her elbow.

"Ow!" he teased. "You must've learned that from

your countrymen, watching them play their lousy excuse for Gaelic football."

Patrick steered them inside a small, family-owned Irish restaurant, which was tucked away on the bottom floor of the apartment building that neighbored the hospital.

Sorcha made a mock gesture of her hand over her heart in exasperation. "If it weren't for corrupt managers and referees, we'd have had the All-Ireland this year."

He wagged a finger at her. "Tsk, tsk. David Clifford would have had the All-Ireland. Kerry still would have been buggered."

Sorcha opened her mouth as if to reply, but then they were inside the restaurant. She stared up at him, a wide smile on her face.

"What is this place?"

"It's Tammy and Aiodhán Sullivan's. They're friends of my family back home and used to have a food cart. They moved here about five years ago."

"How didn't I know this existed?"

"They're a well-kept secret and still usually sell out by the end of lunchtime. It's just local expats who know about it, I think. To be honest, this place is part of the reason this hospital means so much to me. It—" He swallowed the small stone of concern that opening up to Sorcha wasn't the right call. "It's nice having a piece of home nearby."

"You miss it?"

Patrick considered that. He was Irish, through

and through, and Dublin had been his home, Aoife's home. And yet...

"I'm not sure," he answered honestly. "Parts of it for sure."

She nodded, then looked at the sparse menu, inhaling deeply with a smile on her face. Patrick shoved his hands in his trouser pockets to avoid running the heel of his palm down her cheek.

"What should I get?" she asked. When she drew in her bottom lip, her eyes were so uncharacteristically bright he couldn't help but smile, too. Bringing her here was a good move.

"You'd be a right eejit if you didn't have the stew and soda bread, but the pasties are pretty damn fine, as well."

A shadow passed over her face but she recovered her grin.

"Are you okay?" he asked.

She nodded, but her smile fell just enough that he noticed. "My mom used to make stew for us when my sister was sick. She stopped cooking altogether after—" Sorcha nibbled on the corner of her mouth and her eyes watered.

Damn it all, I can't watch her cry and not do anything about it.

Patrick rubbed her back. Was he imagining it, or did she lean into his touch?

"I'm sorry," he said. "We can go—"

"No," she protested. "I'll risk being an eejit for today since I have to get back and line up patients to invite to the trial anyway. A pastie sounds great. Thank you, Patrick, for bringing me here."

"Of course." He'd like to help with whatever trauma was buried beneath her beautiful exterior, what haunted her... But he had things to do before getting even closer to a woman inextricably tied to the past he was trying to move on from.

And you're leaving in seven months.

He wasn't so self-important that he believed it would hurt her if they started something and he flew back to Dublin, but it would crush him to leave her behind. Hell, he already couldn't imagine it, and they'd just broached the beginnings of friendship.

They placed their orders with the couple at the counter, and Sorcha shocked him further when she thanked them in Gaelic.

"Go raibh míle maith agat," she said to Tammy, who came across the counter and took Sorcha's hands in hers. "This place is amazing. I'll be back for sure," she added in English.

"Níl aon tinteán mar do thinteán féin," Tammy replied, her hands clasped over Sorcha's.

"No, there isn't." Sorcha's jaw hardened, but she sent Tammy a sweet smile.

Patrick stared at her until she turned to meet his gaze. Her eyes were lined with grief. It didn't take a medical professional to see the sadness wafting off her in waves.

"I agree there's no place like home," he said. He just didn't know where "home" was right now. "I didn't know you spoke Irish."

"My parents insisted that Cara and I learn. When she passed, I took up the charge. I'd have done anything they asked if it would bring them back to me."

"Did it?"

Sorcha shook her head. "No. We've met up for rare holidays, but it's hard forming a relationship with people who wished you weren't around most of your life."

Patrick's chest constricted like he was seconds away from a myocardial infarction. He put a hand on hers and when she didn't pull away, his heart fluttered. Okay, maybe he was closer to an arrhythmia than anything else.

"I'm sorry that happened to you. You deserved better."

Sorcha met his gaze and something passed between them. He couldn't name it, only felt it. It was as if a brick on the path behind him, the one headed back to Ireland's shores, just crumbled. He felt...unsteady.

"So, have you brought Aoife here?" she asked, finally pulling her hand away. Patrick let her have the topic change. They didn't need to dive into personal waters; he just wanted to spend time with her. Time that was whittling away at a faster clip than he was comfortable with. He could always ask Mick to extend his contract, but how long could he keep Aoife from her homeland? His family?

"I haven't. She actually hates Irish food, the sassy little *cailin*. Boston has ruined her even more with lobster rolls and sushi."

Tammy delivered their food and gave Sorcha a side hug.

Sorcha took a bite of her pastie. "This is delicious," she declared, her gaze trained on Patrick's stew.

"Want to try a bite?" he asked. Her smile brightened the room enough it didn't seem like gloomy Boston awaited them just outside the glass. Then there was the lip bite as she nodded. This woman was going to be the death of him.

"Yes, please."

He scooped a heaping bite onto his spoon and fed her across the table. You wouldn't know he was a world-renowned surgeon the way his hand trembled.

"Er-mer-gerd," she muttered, her mouth full. She swallowed and laughed, wiping at the drip of broth on her lips. Damn if he didn't want to do that for her. With his tongue. Jeez, why couldn't he keep thoughts like that at bay? "That was fabulous."

"Better than your mum's?" he asked.

Her smile didn't falter this time. "Close. Someday, you'll have to taste hers." She dropped her voice to a conspiratorial whisper. "I think even Aoife would like it."

He leaned in, catching a hint of her floral soap. "Well, then, you'll just have to make that happen. I don't think I can head back to Ireland with an Irish lass who won't eat anything but American food."

If he weren't as close to Sorcha's face, he'd have

missed the sharp intake of breath, the dilation of her pupils.

"I almost forgot your job is temporary," she whispered. The words shot straight to Patrick's heart, jolting it like three hundred volts of defibrillator right to the chest. The tips of her fingers met his on the table, barely grazing them. It was a tender enough touch it could have been an accident, but the heat in her eyes, the way the irises turned to liquid jade, said there was more to it. When her feet met his under the table, another zap of electricity shot through his core. She shook her head and straightened. "Well, we'll have to work on reforming her straightaway."

"We will." Patrick opened his mouth to reply but his pager went off, then hers. He frowned. "We need to go. Mick's paging both of us, it seems."

The words he'd been about to say—that if she wanted him to stay, to be there for the trial, for *her*, that he would consider it—were swallowed along with the stew he inhaled.

How was it that this woman, this frustratingly beautiful, serious woman he'd never even kissed, was making him forget not only his past, but his plans to return home?

Seven hells, she was making him forget the *definition* of the word *home*. Suddenly, it sounded a lot like a stormy night in the city, the paper wrapping from lobster rolls in the trash, the three of them cuddled up on the couch watching American TV shows.

The first order after dinner was figuring out why Mick had ruined a perfectly tender, vulnerable moment with a string of after-hours pages. It damn well better be an emergency awaiting them. Nothing less was a good enough excuse for pulling Patrick out of Sorcha's orbit. Not even the work piling up on his desk.

"Okay," she said, eating the last of her pie, "I'll follow you."

As Patrick used the pad of his thumb to wipe a crumb from her lip, he wondered, *How far?*

CHAPTER ELEVEN

SORCHA GLARED AT her phone as she placed her empty plate in the bus bin of the small restaurant. The three notifications were from Mick: the first congratulated her, the second wondered where she was and the third wanted to meet—immediately, if possible.

She shot back a reply.

At dinner.

When her phone buzzed twice more, she sighed.

We're almost there. Had to finish eating before we came back to work.

Which is after-hours as it is, she wanted to add. Sorcha strode through the door, holding it open for Patrick. Trial numbers ran through her head on the off chance Mick quizzed her. Anything to avoid wondering why the electricity buzzing between her and Patrick was strong enough to send a three-hundred-pound man into cardiac arrest.

Twenty-four patients to start. Three subsets of

eight. First eight get the trial treatment and medication. Second eight get the treatment sans meds, and the last eight get the placebo.

Her gut churned at that last set of numbers. Placebos were a mandated part of every trial as a control group, but it didn't make it any easier to think about the children, the families, who wouldn't get the life-saving treatment Sorcha's trial promised. The families knew what they were getting into when they signed up for the trial, but still... At least, at the end of it all, when her plan was approved, she'd never have to turn patients away again.

"Can I ask you something?" Patrick queried, slowing to a stop outside the maternity ward. Sorcha gazed at the babies in incubators, little pieces of joy and hope living outside their parents' bodies. Love tethered them to their families, but Sorcha knew the darker underbelly to that cord.

Fear.

She rubbed her chest. The proximity to the tiny swaddled bundles of Sorcha's worst anxieties made her skin itch as if she'd developed an allergy to connection, to love.

In a way, she had. It was sort of like a chocoholic finding out they couldn't have sugar anymore, though. She *desperately* wanted a family, cords tying her to others who could rely on her, who she could rely on.

Patrick had shown her that truth. Which meant she didn't want just anyone; for better or worse, she wanted him and Aoife—the family she'd inadvertently made over the past couple months.

But how was that possible? What she saw every day—the loss, the pain, the crevasse of grief that swallowed families whole? If she let that in, yes, she'd get the best parts of family—connection, support, and love. But the rest came with it, and she still hadn't figured out how to cope with that.

Her job was the only thing she could rely on; it was all she had.

Was it?

She turned her back to the nursery window and faced Patrick.

"Sure," she replied.

Patrick took her hand in his. "I'm not asking you this as your boss, or the guy who promised you funding. I'm asking as a—" He glanced down at his feet. Was Patrick Quinn nervous? "A friend. Would you show Aoife and me around? It's been a bit since I've been here, and I'm woefully unprepared for having a kid in Boston. I keep taking her to the same three places."

As a friend.

She wasn't allowed to feel the tightening in her abdomen, or the flutter in her chest when she looked at him. She definitely wasn't allowed to dream about his crooked smile, or those lips on hers. All that was too close to "longing," which was on her "do not take" medication list.

But being friends was okay. Sorcha smiled. At

least she had him in her life in some small way. It had to be enough.

"I'd like that." She pulled back her hand when she realized the heat between their palms wasn't very "friendly."

"I did promise Aoife I'd take her somewhere."

Patrick smiled, his eyes glittering with mischief.

"And where did my darling daughter demand you take her?"

Sorcha bit her lip. "In her words, she wants to see the leprechauns who throw the ball in the basket. The ones with the four-leaf clovers on their hats."

Patrick coughed.

"My daughter wants to go to a Celtics game?" Sorcha nodded. "Does she know what it is?"

"I tried to tell her, but she wouldn't listen. She said fairies and leprechauns talk and since she hadn't heard from her fairies since she'd arrived, it was important we go so she could chat with the leprechauns. Something about that list she showed us the other night?"

The color left Patrick's cheeks.

"Jeez. I didn't know she was hearing things now. Should I get her checked out?"

It was Sorcha's turn to laugh. "She's fine. She's just being four."

"What's her age got to do with it?"

"There isn't a child I work with who didn't bring an imaginary friend or two with them to surgery. And I don't think Aoife talks to them as much as wishes on them. I'll admit I did the same when I was young."

"To save your sister?" he asked.

She nodded, glad he understood. "And then to bring me another sister when the first request didn't work out." Sorcha tucked her hands into her lab coat pockets. It didn't hurt so much as ache in the place Cara lived in her heart. "The very next week Rachel sat next to me on the bus on the way to school. The first question she asked was if I believed in guardian angels. I taught her about Irish fairies and, well, the rest is history. I got the sister I asked for in the end."

Another ache, another loss. One Patrick confronted her with every time he smiled at her. Which was another reason all she could be was his friend—no matter how he made her feel.

"Rachel never told me that. But I see where Aoife gets it now. It's in the family all the way back to you."

Sorcha pushed through the steel doors of the surgical wing, ignoring the casual mention of her being part of Patrick and Aoife's family. Thankfully it was loud enough in the hallway he probably couldn't hear the way her heart slammed hard against her rib cage.

"Anyway," she said, desperate for a subject change, "how do you feel about basketball?"

Patrick's lips parted as Sorcha walked through the vacuum of space between the old part of the wing and where the new floor was being built.

Whatever he'd been about to say was interrupted by loud shouting behind them. A high-pitched whistle rang against the steel door and she startled, losing her balance. Time slowed and the air seemed to still as she fell backward. Bracing herself, she waited for the crack of her head on the door. But it never came.

Instead, she found herself hitting a wall—of hard, sculpted flesh, anyway. Patrick's arms wrapped around her body, steadying her. Her pulse and blood pressure skyrocketed, wildly out of control, especially when his hands rested on her hips, righting her after her near fall.

Sorcha's breath hitched in her chest. Was Patrick's thumb caressing her hip bone, or did she imagine it? Either way, the perception of it, coupled with her imagination that ran rogue picturing what his hands might feel like on other parts of her—*all* of her—made her stomach dip.

"Um…thanks," she said. His breath was warm on her skin but still served to give her goose bumps. "I thought I was a goner."

"I'd never let anything happen to you, Sorcha," he said. His voice was thick and gravelly, as if he had something stuck in his throat. The thing was, she believed him. He'd been saving her left and right since they'd met.

Friends. We can only be friends.

The mantra felt shallow and without the same weight as before.

"Patrick, I—"

"Congratulations, Sorcha!" voices called out. She lifted her head and the blood rushed to her skin, while the whole surgery department stared at them.

She wriggled free and noticed the "Congratulations!" banner above the small crowd of nurses and surgeons. Even a few board members were there.

"What's this?" she asked. Although, as she recovered from the initial shock, she got it.

Patrick had taken her out to distract her.

The banner. The crowd...

She was at her first surprise party.

"We're celebrating your trial being approved," Mick called out. His eyes darted between her and Patrick, trying to work out what he'd just witnessed. "It was darn near impossible to pull off this surprise with you holed up in your office this afternoon, I'll tell ya that much. I thought we had it in the bag when you started spending nights and weekends—" he glanced at Patrick "—away."

Sorcha put on the most crowd-friendly smile she could muster. How much did Mick know about her free time spent with Aoife and Patrick? It wasn't like she'd done anything untoward, but Patrick was still her boss.

"Thanks, Mick. This is, er, great. What a surprise."

He grinned and pulled her into a bear hug. "You deserve it. I've never seen anyone work as hard as you. Until this guy came along," he joked, slapping Patrick on the shoulder with his free hand. "And it's a big win for the hospital. Some red tape to jump through with the board's allocation of funding, but this approval was an important step."

"Is the red tape anything to worry about?" Sorcha asked.

"Shouldn't be. But leave that to me. Right now, you two enjoy yourselves."

"Sorcha, congratulations. Unfortunately, I've got some work to do. But Mick's right. You deserve this." Patrick turned to leave.

"Nonsense, Dr. Quinn," Mick said. "You're not on call. Get yourself a piece of cake and some champagne. I insist. Sorcha, come with me and I'll introduce you to some of the board."

"Actually, can I chat with you real quick, Dr. Quinn?" Sorcha asked. When Mick sighed like he was testing his lungs with a spirometer, she glared at him. "I'll be there in a sec."

Mick nodded and joined the other surgeons around what looked like a makeshift bar.

Patrick turned to Sorcha. "Is everything okay?" he asked her. The concern in his voice was clear. She had her own to sift through, though.

"I don't know," she answered honestly. "Were you—were you part of this?" she asked. Her skin itched, imagining that the only reason she'd been asked to share an intimate dinner with Patrick was to keep her occupied so the surprise could be pulled off. That, coupled with him submitting her trial paperwork on her behalf, made her feel...

As if her life were being lived *for* her, rather than her living it.

His eyes deepened in color, turning a deep sea-green like the Atlantic after a winter storm.

"No, *bean álainn*, I wasn't. I only wanted to go to dinner with you. Apparently we were both tricked."

The blush deepened enough she could feel the heat emanating from her skin.

"Oh." She swallowed hard. "You really didn't know about the party?"

Patrick's frown answered. "No. And I'm not sure why I wasn't invited. Mick knows we've been spending time with each other."

Sorcha's mouth fell open. "He does?"

"Of course. I wanted to be honest with him in case—" He shook his head and then met her gaze as if he was willing her to finish his sentence for him. She didn't dare in case her answer was off base enough to drive their new friendship away. "Anyway. No, I wasn't involved in the surprise."

His mind seemed to be whirring, his body torn between fleeing the scene and taking part in the festivities. His eyes darkened into jade stones before he grabbed her hand. All the blood that had pooled in her cheeks dropped to her stomach. People could *see*.

"Let's make the most of it, then," he said. "Starting with a drink. What do you say?"

What *could* she say? The man might have a hold of her hand, leading her through the crowd to the bar, but she would have followed him anyway. That secret she kept close to her heart, but it still felt like all the world could see it as easily as she wore a blush.

"Okay," she said. "Let's celebrate then. I'm buying," she teased.

CHAPTER TWELVE

AT SOME POINT, Patrick glanced up and realized the party was winding down.

"We're real party animals, aren't we?" Sorcha asked.

Patrick smiled and tucked a red curl behind her ear. Her skin matched the color of her hair, and he longed to feel the heat from her cheeks in the palm of his hand.

Sorcha hiccupped. "'Scuse me," she murmured.

A thrill whispered against Patrick's heart. And it wasn't just the champagne talking, either. He genuinely *liked* the woman, try as he had to avoid that more than minor complication.

"I must've had one too many wines."

Patrick grinned. "You've only had two. But we should probably get you home," he said.

"Thank you, Patrick. You know," she said, "you're kinda cute when you're not being an Irish know-it-all."

He swallowed a laugh since she seemed rather serious.

"Is that a fact?" She nodded. The woman was

definitely scuttered. It was a relief to see her with her hair down, metaphorically speaking. "What is the difference between an Irish and American know-it-all?"

She scrunched up her lips into what could have passed as thoughtful if she weren't leaning to the left. A finger jabbed him in the chest.

"An American know-it-all doesn't actually know anything. And they don't have a sexy accent."

A single nod acted as punctuation. So, Sorcha found him both cute and sexy? *Hmm.* The information shouldn't make any difference to him, but somehow...he couldn't stop wondering what else she thought of him. They'd come a long way since he'd stolen her job, but was it too much to ask that she be as interested in him outside of work as he was in her?

But even if she was...what was he prepared to do about it? Memories of Rachel lingered just underneath his growing feelings for Sorcha, clouding them.

When Sorcha leaned on his shoulder, those feelings pushed the rest away. Patrick made a mental note that two tall glasses of champagne were the sweet spot to get Sorcha Kelly chatting. He nodded to Mick.

"I'm taking this one home. To her home, I mean. Then I'm going back to my place."

He cringed.

"Have a good night, Dr. Quinn," Mick said with a wink.

Patrick had texted the sitter he'd be late and she'd shot back to take his time; Aoife was asleep. Thank goodness for public transport since he'd had two glasses of wine as well. Holding Sorcha's hand, he meandered out of the hospital and into the cool spring night toward the train station.

When they got off a couple of stops later, the winds had died down and there was a hint of something floral hanging in the air. In a few weeks, the eastern redbud and cherry trees would be in full bloom. Spring was here, meaning there were only two more seasons for him in Boston. At the end of the year, he and Aoife would head back to Ireland, leaving their past behind them for good.

The wind wasn't the only thing that had calmed. This late on a weeknight, there weren't horns blaring, or shop owners yelling. Only the gentle hum of the city that had nurtured, helping him become the physician and surgeon that he was.

Even Sorcha had stilled, taking deep breaths that seemed to sober her. Watching the corners of her mouth turn up as she faced the city she called home, he couldn't help but wonder—when he left, would he be leaving more than just his past behind?

"Have I told you how much I hated Boston when I was a kid?" she asked. He shook his head. "For years I thought it was a punishment for wishing my sister would get better so we could go back to Castlemaine. But now…it's grown on me." She inhaled with relish. "It smells like the inside of a flower shop," Sorcha said. "God, spring in this city is fantastic. Everything feels alive."

Patrick squeezed her hand. "It is grand, isn't it? Dublin's nice and all, but spring doesn't come till late June and by then, we're all just anxiously awaiting the one week a year we're able to hide away our slickers."

"Ah, I see where you've been tucking away your Irish slang, Dr. Quinn. Does it just take a couple of glasses of wine to bring it out?"

"Now that you mention it, I didn't really notice how much I hide my true self here. Rachel didn't understand half the things I said when we first moved to Dublin, so I think over time I carved 'em out to make room for her."

Sorcha slid up beside him again, her eyes glittering under the streetlights. "My friend was one of the best women in the world, but yer girl didn't much appreciate feelin' like an outsider."

"Not so much."

She grinned—the kind of smile he'd seen on her face in the lab when she got a result she'd been hoping for. Seeing it aimed at him sent flashes of heat from his core to his chest. And south.

Only a small pang of guilt accompanied the sensation. Talking about Rachel with a woman he'd imagined taking up her side of the bed was something he didn't think he'd get used to. It was made all the worse by knowing Sorcha and the woman had been best friends.

Even though he'd thought about dating when he

got back to Dublin, starting that off with a woman who had her own complicated feelings about his late wife felt like a betrayal.

But not enough of one to ignore the pull of his heart when she took his hand again.

"I think she had it all wrong." His stomach tightened. Could she feel the electricity buzzing against the polarities of their palms? Or was he imagining it?

He swallowed hard, tried like hell to remember why he'd felt guilty about something that felt this *good*.

"How's that?"

Patrick held his breath when Sorcha leaned in. "I think you're a right eejit for hiding who you are or where you come from, even for a second. Just be yourself, Patrick. There are those of us who'll love you for it all the same."

Love? Did she mean her? Forget his stomach tightening; it was in pure knots now.

"Um…thanks. And I'll try."

In the midst of the suddenly serious conversation, he hadn't realized they'd arrived home. Not Sorcha's, as he'd promised, but *his*. Sorcha had led him there and he'd let her. That was the only explanation for the fact that she was walking up his stairs, his hand still in hers. And he was following her without so much as an argument.

Any guilt he'd felt earlier must've floated away on the breeze. It was freeing, but he'd be lying if he didn't feel a hint of danger where the trepidation had once been.

"What're you doing?" he asked. He barely recognized his own voice it was so thick.

"Taking you home," she answered. He eked out a nod.

"Dropping me off?" he countered.

She shook her head, biting her bottom lip. Her thumb caressed the pad of his palm and goose bumps shot up his arm.

When her gaze dipped to his mouth, he didn't have any questions about what she wanted. And hell—he wanted it, too. Like chest-pounding, shout-from-the-rooftop wanted it. Wanted *her*. But...

"We've had a couple of drinks tonight, Sorch."

"I know what I'm doing." And with that, she closed the gap between them. She still wore her white lab coat, her name inscribed above the pocket—*Dr. Sorcha Kelly*, a name he'd known as long as he'd known Rachel. But the way *he* knew it wasn't tied at all to his late wife. It was his own, private knowledge.

For a split second, he imagined her jacket read *Dr. Sorcha Quinn*, and before his head got the message, his heart decided he liked that as much as he liked her palm pressed against his, as much as he appreciated her laugh, rare as it was. As much as he adored watching Sorcha and Aoife chat about fairies.

And that was all he needed to dip his chin and meet her lips.

When their mouths met, his hands—and the rest of his body—seemed to know precisely what to do. So he let them. He didn't overthink the way his fingers tangled in her crimson curls, or how soft they were. He didn't worry about how his hips pressed into hers, desperate to be as close to her as possible.

He especially didn't concern himself with the flame blossoming where their lips touched and spreading out from there like wildfire. Let him burn to ash if it felt this good, this satisfying, this—

Perfect. It's never felt this right before.

When guilt didn't follow at that admission, his lips parted and his tongue explored the curve of her lips, the shape of her mouth. She tasted like sugar and champagne, and it was enough to bring back his buzz, or at least the lightheaded giddiness he'd felt earlier.

Sorcha deepened the kiss, wrapping her arms tighter around his neck and pulling him close. Her tongue met his and he wasn't sure who moaned—maybe both of them at the same time—but he wanted her right then and there.

He slid his other hand down her back, around to her hip. Now it was definitely Sorcha who groaned with pleasure as his thumb slid between the fabric of her shirt and skin. He gripped her hip and ground into her.

"Patrick," she whispered into his mouth. His name on her lips was the second sexiest thing about her.

A dog barked somewhere behind them and whatever spell he'd been under broke. He was making out with a woman on his doorstep? The reality of their situation left him aware of just how close he'd been to damaging more than his memories of Rachel. He risked his reputation at the hospital, and so much more.

His heart, and Aoife's for one.

Patrick pulled back, breathless. This was wrong... wasn't it?

Why didn't it seem that way, despite every reason it should be?

He needed distance. Space to think.

As if anything but running back to Ireland would be enough to forget that kiss.

"Holy—" he started, extracting the hand from her mess of curls and running it through his own hair. "We, uh, *wow*."

"For a man who's fluent in two languages and has an advanced degree, that's...one way to describe what we were doing."

She bit the corner of her bottom lip and every time she'd been stubborn, or frustrated seemed impossible now in the face of her smiling up at him like *that*.

"Yeah, I guess so. I'm just not sure what to say."

"Say you'll take me upstairs and finish what we started."

"Sorcha, I—"

Her eyes narrowed and her smile faltered.

"It's fine," she said, shrugging. For a self-assured woman at work, he was well aware of her insecurities in her personal life. *Damn.* He'd only been considering how he felt about kissing her, not what it would mean for her to give him that kind of trust. He'd really stepped in it, hadn't he? "You're right. We have a busy week ahead of us. Thanks for dinner, Patrick."

She leaned up and pecked him on the cheek before turning away and walking down the stairs.

"Wait," he called out, jumping down to the sidewalk in one leap. For the second time that night, he shut his mind off and let his body lead the way.

"Yes?" she asked. The hope in her voice was answer enough.

"I only hesitated because I want to make sure you really want this," he said. It was partly true. His body cashed in on the rest of the lie. She was in his arms again before he could reason his way out of them.

"I do," she whispered. "More than you know."

"If we do this," he began, his last attempt at sanity before he let this blaze consume him, "we can't let it get in the way of work."

"My thoughts exactly. Or your parenting. Aoife is what matters most. Even if I'm saying that through a lustful haze, I mean it."

Patrick stared at Sorcha. He believed her, that wasn't the problem. The issue was, he'd never been so turned on in his life. Sorcha hadn't just said Aoife mattered, she'd been *proving* it day after day as she helped him with his lack of childcare and then went above and beyond caring for his daughter in a way she'd been missing nearly her whole life.

And damn if that wasn't one of the sexiest things about Sorcha.

Leaving his arm around her waist, he escorted her up the stairs again. "Then, Dr. Kelly, will you come up to my place?"

"I'd like that," she whispered, leaning up and planting a kiss on his cheek. "Take me to bed, Dr. Quinn."

And that's the only thing Patrick thought about on the longest elevator ride he'd ever endured, through paying the babysitter and kissing his sleeping daughter good night.

When he came out to the living room of the apartment, Sorcha had shed her coat. Her hair was mussed, the curls and heat evidence of their earlier make out session on the stoop.

Her bottom lip was drawn between her teeth and the way she gazed up at him, eyes wide and bright, well…it was safe to say he'd never been as attracted to anyone. Ever. He let the full weight of what that meant fall to his feet.

It didn't change the love he'd felt for his wife— nothing could. But it did irrevocably alter the shame and guilt around that love and loss.

"You're beautiful," he said, taking her hand in his. Heat spread down her neck, a map of desire he wanted to follow as it meandered south.

"Shh. I don't know if you heard me out there, Patrick, but I'm a sure thing."

"That doesn't mean I can't tell you how I feel, now does it?"

She shook her head. More than likely, she wasn't the subject of much flattery locked away in her lab each day.

He threaded his fingers through her hair, cupping the base of her head. Drawing her in for a kiss, he whispered, "And you're sexy." She shivered in his grasp. He kissed her again. "You're also the most brilliant woman I've ever met." A moan this time, from deep in her chest. He kissed her a third time. "And you're the hottest doctor on the planet. Including those actors on *Grey's Anatomy.*"

Sorcha giggled, but when he dipped down a fourth time, his lips brushing hers and his hands sliding down her back, her breath hitched in her chest.

Patrick cupped her butt, drawing her closer. She gasped. "Tell me what you want. I want to give you everything you desire, Sorcha."

To prove it, he traced his lips and teeth along her neck. The sigh of pleasure that escaped her lips said he was off to a good start.

"That. Keep doing that."

Pulling down the fabric of her blouse, he traced her collarbone with his tongue.

"I—I haven't done this…" she breathed out. "I haven't done this in a while. I need you to take the lead. Please," she added.

"As you wish," he said. Cradling her in his arms, he didn't stop kissing her as he made his way to his bedroom. He set her on the bed and knelt in front of her. "Lift your arms for me," he instructed.

She obliged, and he pulled her blouse over her head. Her arms fell around his neck, but her eyes did, too.

"Look at me, Sorcha." Patrick tipped up her chin until her gaze met his. "I need to see you."

She held his gaze and he reached around, unclasping her bra. Her full breasts fell into his eager hands and damn if it wasn't all he could do not to come right then and there.

"Lie back," he told her. Sorcha nodded and lay on the mattress. He spread her legs and slid his hands and gaze down her curvy frame, marveling at her perfection. She arched her back when he teased her nipples between his thumb and finger.

"Lift your hips," Patrick growled. When she did, he unbuttoned her slacks and slid them off. His lips continued down her taut stomach and she gasped when his tongue traced her panty line.

God… His chest was tight with want, and his own pants were snug along the zipper. There was no way one woman could hold so much passion for others, such physical beauty, and such intelligence. It shouldn't be possible, but as he pulled her underwear down and his mouth pressed between her legs, he realized it was.

Sorcha Kelly was everything he'd ever wanted. At the absolute worst time for him to realize it. But that was neither here nor there. Not when *this* moment was in front of him.

"You're beautiful," he whispered, his chin resting on her thigh. She tried to shake her head, but he wasn't having any of that. He dipped his lips and thrust his tongue inside her folds, desperate to show her just how much he wanted her, how wonderful she was.

"Oh, Patrick," she moaned.

He sucked and pulled at her center until her breathing quickened.

"I—" she started. He flicked her tight core with his tongue. "Oh! Oh, God."

That was more like it. Sorcha did everything for everyone else. This was something he could give back. Something just for her pleasure. Patrick cupped Sorcha's butt and brought her hips to the edge of the bed. He swirled his tongue inside her, tasting and appreciating the brine that reminded him of the salt on his lips after a swim in the Irish Sea. He picked up his pace until her hips bucked and her knees tightened around his head.

"Yes," she called out. "I'm coming. So…close."

Patrick squeezed her backside and redoubled his efforts until her thighs spasmed and she released a cry of such exquisite pleasure all he could do was grin, his lips still pressed to her.

"Oh, Patrick," she whispered, her body still quivering. "I want—"

"Yes?" he asked. He'd give her just about anything, a realization that only mildly surprised him.

"I want *you*. Make love to me, Patrick."

"It's about damn time," he laughed. "I was hoping you'd come to yer senses and boss me around for a change."

She laughed, and as he stood in front of her, disrobing and sheathing himself with a condom, he wasn't sure he'd ever been happier. Or that he'd want to leave that happiness behind for a half life in Dublin.

And that *did* surprise him.

CHAPTER THIRTEEN

PATRICK'S EYES OPENED just enough to find the source of the pale light. *Aha.* He'd forgotten to shut the windows last night. The hint of dawn approached, and with it, a reminder of why he'd been so distracted the evening before.

Sorcha. In his home. His bed. *Finally.*

He stretched his arm out to bring her closer, only to find that side of the bed cool and empty. What the—

He sat up. Sorcha was climbing into her slacks, her blouse still thankfully missing. Memories of those perfect, full breasts in his hands, his mouth...

"Come back to bed," he growled, his body strung tight with lust again, as if they hadn't made love most of the night.

She squeaked with surprise, startling and almost falling as well. "I've got to go before Aoife wakes up. We didn't talk about...*after.*"

He patted the space beside him. "I'd like to, if you're okay pausing your stealthy exit for a minute."

She glowered at him in much the same way as when he'd been announced as the interim chief.

Only this time, the corners of her lips quirked with the hint of a smile. "Fine. But only for a minute. She gets up early on nonschool days so she can have more time to play."

Was that true? He guessed it was, but in sharing parenting time with Sorcha, he'd overlooked some of the details of his daughter's life. It was nice, knowing she was cared for, but he didn't want to get complacent, either.

Sorcha sat beside him, and he wrapped an arm around her bare waist. It took all his self-control not to pull her on top of him and ravage her while he could. For some reason it felt like if she left, whatever magic had occurred the night before would evaporate.

Maybe it was high time he started asking the fairies for things of his own.

"Thank you for spending so much time with Aoife. You've been a blessing I never expected, Sorcha."

"Of course. She's amazing, Patrick. You've done a great job with her."

"I appreciate you saying so. She's a feisty one— her mother's daughter to be sure."

"It breaks my heart Rachel never got to see her grow up."

Patrick nodded, but the heat that used to build in his chest whenever he thought about that never came. He'd grieved the choice she'd made to refuse treatment, grieved her, grieved the future they were supposed to have together.

Now it was time for him to *live* again. What that life would look like, he couldn't say with certainty, only that last night's events confirmed he wanted it to include Sorcha.

One question remained, though.

"Where do you sit with Rachel?" he asked. Her eyes went wide, and she covered her chest protectively. "I think we're past pretending I haven't seen or tasted those perfect breasts," he teased. She smiled and he used the levity to pull her down onto his chest. "I want us to be able to talk about her, but I understand if that's difficult," he added. Sorcha's head fit perfectly in the nook between his shoulder and chest. Her finger rubbed lazy circles on his chest.

"It's okay. It's just—" She lifted her head to look at him. "I hated you for so long for thinking you kept her from me, from her family."

That wasn't what he'd expected. There didn't seem to be guilt about sleeping with him, just hurt feelings about their complicated friendship.

"I know. You're not alone, you know. Her parents still want me dead." He grimaced.

"I believe it. Still, I'm sorry. I should have reached out to both of you. Life's too short for holding grudges."

Patrick kissed the top of Sorcha's head, inhaling her scent and committing it to memory. As if he'd forget even one minute of this…

"I get why you hated me, but why did you and Rachel fall out?" he asked.

"My parents and I were estranged at that point. They didn't approve of my choice of career—not when they'd 'done everything' to keep Cara and me out of hospitals."

Sorcha sniffled against his chest, and he felt the dampness where tears must be falling. He ran his fingers through her hair.

"When I got into medical school—my top choice—Rachel was supposed to help me move since my folks weren't answering my calls. Just like she was supposed to come with me to see my favorite rock band, The Frames, when we were in college. Like she was supposed to be my roommate in college."

The sun peeked over the edge of the horizon through the open windows. They were talking on borrowed time. Aoife would be up any minute. He could only pursue Sorcha with Aoife's full understanding and approval since her life would be irrevocably altered if this new thing with Sorcha went anywhere, but he wanted—needed—to take it slow where his daughter was concerned. And selfishly, he wanted Sorcha to himself as he got to know her in this way.

"Instead, she moved to Ireland with me that weekend, didn't she?" Sorcha nodded. "I'm so sorry. I never knew. She told me that you didn't understand her, but that you'd come around."

"I didn't understand her, that much is true." She paused. "Do you mind hearing this? She was your wife, and I know you loved her."

Patrick considered that. At one point, he'd have defended Rachel to the last of his days. But Sorcha knew her as well as he did—maybe better in some respects. That they shared her should have made things more complicated, but really, it only brought him closer to Sorcha.

"She was and I did. Deeply. But she was your best friend, too."

"Thank you. Anyway, Rachel had a family who loved and supported her, passion enough to pursue anything, and yet it felt like she was always…"

"Running away?" Patrick suggested. Sorcha nodded again. "I know. It was one of our constant fights, the way she gave up immediately if things didn't go her way. Rachel was a lot of things, but persistent wasn't one of them."

Until the end.

"She was my only real family and she left me. I was so hurt, Patrick, but I still should have tried to fix things between us. Friendship should be reciprocal, but maybe expecting her to reciprocate in the same way I did wasn't entirely fair. It wasn't who Rachel was. God love her, but she danced to her own jig."

"She did, didn't she?" It was a perfect way to describe his late wife. The desire to tell Sorcha he could reciprocate, wanted to give her back all she'd given him, almost choked him. But something blocked the words from leaving his mouth.

Just when he'd thought he'd fully opened up to her.

The guilt Patrick had felt about pursuing Sorcha,

his wife's estranged friend, released its hold on his heart now that her complex feelings about Rachel were out in the open, but the words still didn't come. He tipped Sorcha's head up and kissed her with everything he couldn't say. Deeply, passionately, and with all the understanding that their time with Rachel was left unfulfilled.

So why couldn't he find the words to tell Sorcha how amazing she was, or what he wanted?

A thought smashed against the back of his skull, almost breaking their kiss.

Because, when you invite another person into your life, how can you trust they'll involve you in theirs when things get tough? Is that why you turned in her trial paperwork? So there wouldn't be anything "tough" to go through with her?

Damn. He hadn't thought of it that way. Maybe.

But Sorcha wasn't Rachel, obviously; they could talk about the tough stuff.

Well, she could. He'd get there, too, in time.

Patrick kissed her again, this time softly, tenderly letting her know he was there, he heard her, and cared for her. When she shifted off him and wiped away a stray tear, his heart clenched.

"So, um, want to go grab breakfast?" she said. "I could pretend to come back over. We could take Aoife to a movie or something after."

His eyes widened. "Oh, I…"

"Sorry. I didn't mean to assume."

"No. That's not why I hesitated. I want to spend

as much time with you as I can. There's just some-thing I have to do first."

The truth hit him square in the chest. He'd come to Boston with two goals—to say a final goodbye to Rachel, and to introduce Aoife to her grandpar-ents. And he hadn't done either. But somehow, he'd let himself develop feelings for another woman. No wonder he couldn't tell Sorcha how he felt; he was still tethered to his past.

Just a little while longer…

"That works. I'm sorry if you think I'm rushing things. I'm just a little out of practice with—" she waved a hand between her half-naked self and his fully nude one "—this."

He leaned in again and kissed her.

"Me, too. But I like what we're doing."

"So do I." She got up and finished dressing, and he kissed her one last time at the door before she left. God, it was hard to watch her walk away, to leave his sight. That had to count for something, didn't it?

Patrick shook his head and went to Aoife's room. She was just stretching in bed, her hair a tangled mess of curls.

"Hello, *mo grá*," he said, giving her a hug. "How did you sleep?"

"Mmm… Good. I had dreams about the fairies again." Her smile was still sleepy, her eyes half-shut. "I think they finally got my letters."

"Oh, yeah?" Aoife nodded. "Why's that?"

She shrugged. "I heard Sorcha's voice. She's the one, Da. For you and me."

Patrick's heart pounded in his chest. "What about Ma?" Aoife had mentioned a new mother for herself before, but never a person for *him*. That she might understand the distinction, even a little, gave him hope. It also unlocked a new challenge—walking the line between the past and future with his young daughter. He wanted to show her where she came from but also where they could go. It was a tall order.

"I loved Ma, didn't I?" she said.

"Of course you did."

"And I love Sorcha, too. Can't I love two people at the same time?"

Patrick's throat threatened to close altogether. "Um, yeah, you can." Which meant…he could, too. Something cracked in his chest, letting in light. "I want to talk more about this, but can you do me a favor and get dressed pretty quick? I want to take you to meet some people."

"Mommy's people?"

Patrick smiled. "How did you know?"

She shrugged. "You told me we would when we got here."

He laughed and ruffled her hair. "You're too smart for your own good, love."

Aoife hopped out of bed, dragging the stuffed bunny rabbit Sorcha had bought behind her.

"Please let this go okay," Patrick whispered into the ether. Whether his words were meant for some higher power or Aoife's fairies, he didn't know. Only that he meant them with every cell in his body. His future depended on it.

Two hours later, Patrick and Aoife were both sitting uncomfortably in overstuffed chairs in the Walkers' living room.

And no, it was not going well.

Rachel's parents had agreed to meet them at their home, but hadn't said they were excited to see him and Aoife.

When they'd arrived, he'd seen why.

Joanna was a mess. She'd headed right for them, arms outstretched, and Aoife's face had lit up like she was under OR lights. But Joanna had bypassed Aoife and held her hands out for Patrick to put Rachel's urn in them.

Aoife had gazed up at him with hurt and surprise, and if he were a smart man, he'd have left. But these people had lost a daughter, and he knew grief did some pretty heinous stuff normal pathology couldn't explain.

But so far, all Patrick had accomplished was repeatedly answering Joanna's pleas to share Rachel's last words with her. David had demanded Patrick walk him through Rachel's diagnosis and treatment, wondered out loud why Patrick hadn't brought her "home to the States," and then had the audacity to openly blame Patrick for not being the surgeon to operate on Rachel's tumor.

"That's not how it works," Patrick had responded.

"It's a massive conflict of interest to operate on family."

"Sure it is. Or it's a crime not to take your loved one's care into your own hands. You see it your way, we see it ours."

Patrick raked his hands down his cheeks.

"Aoife drew you a picture," he said. "Go ahead and show them, *mo grá*." Aoife, glad to be mentioned, held it up.

David accepted the paper, a crayon rendering of their family, with Rachel as an angel bearing wings, and the addition of a puppy and fairy to round off the image. It was so absolutely his daughter that Patrick smiled despite the atmosphere in the room.

"How old are you?" David asked Aoife without meeting her gaze. Patrick's shoulders tensed. Was this man finally realizing he had a flesh and blood granddaughter right in front of him?

"I'm four. But I can read already." She sat tall, poised, her shoulders back and smile proud.

Patrick wanted to wrap her in a hug and add that she wasn't just a reader, she was wicked intelligent, fun-loving, and the most caring girl he knew and should be as proud of herself as he was to be her da.

"Four," David whispered, glancing back at his wife, who hadn't said much of anything other than short whispers to the urn in her lap. "I can't believe she's been gone nearly that long."

Patrick's lips pressed flat. David and Joanna might be grieving, but they were also selfish, unfeeling, and blind if they couldn't see the darling girl yearning for their attention.

"Is this my mum?" Aoife asked. She reached for the photo on the table next to her chair.

David reached out and slapped her hand away. "Don't touch that," he growled.

Aoife pulled her hand back, and though the contact had been swift and not terribly strong, her eyes brimmed with tears. Patrick had never laid a hand on her, and never would.

"Come here, *mo grá*." He pulled her into his lap. "Why don't you go play with Misty outside?" he suggested.

She nodded and skipped toward the family dog in the backyard as if nothing was amiss. God love his daughter with her innocent trust so easily repaired. When she was safely out of earshot, he wheeled on David. "Because you lost a daughter, I'll forgive you for laying a hand on mine. But don't *ever* think you'll get away with that again."

There was fire in David's eyes, but also pain. Patrick had released his own agony in order to care for and love Aoife the way she deserved, but reckoned if he hadn't, he'd look the same.

"She looks just like her, doesn't she?" David asked. His shoulders were slumped, and Patrick felt a wave of sorrow for the lost and broken man.

"She does. She's got Rachel's strength, too. If it weren't for her hair and eyes, I wouldn't be sure she was mine at all," Patrick replied.

Silence spanned the gap between the two men,

punctuated by soft sobs from Joanna in the corner as she clung to the remains of her daughter. It wasn't as if Patrick didn't empathize; if anything ever happened to Aoife, he didn't know how he'd survive it. But David and Joanna had each other, and a grandchild, too, yet couldn't see beyond their grief to welcome those gifts.

Patrick's thoughts went to Sorcha, to the photo of her and Rachel on her desk at work. Even back then, in tattered jeans and fire-red hair wild in the breeze, she'd looked serious, like the world wasn't what she'd thought it was. She'd grown up with parents so wrapped up in their own guilt and grief they'd forgotten to raise her. And yet, in spite of them, she'd grown into a selfless, driven, beautiful woman. Serious, yes, but he'd seen her relax into childlike wonder at fairies, collapse into a fit of giggles with his daughter, too.

He had a new appreciation for Sorcha. For what she offered his daughter—despite not being a blood relation, she was taking the place of Aoife's family. For what she offered *him* just by making him feel emotions he'd thought were extinct.

Hell, if he were being honest, he'd never felt as safe and inspired by a woman in his life. Not even Rachel. It didn't mean he hadn't loved her wholeheartedly, just that it'd been different because *he'd* been different. Younger, less inclined to notice what sustained a relationship—trust, communication, and passion in equal measures. They hadn't had the time to learn about true connection and love before it was too late.

A flash of guilt splashed him. He hated that feeling, that he might have let his wife down by not loving her as deeply as he was able. But at the same time, he let it wash over him; he'd done the best he could at the time. If he was lucky enough to get a second chance at love, he'd learn from his mistakes.

"Son, I appreciate you bringing her here—both of 'em. But it's…" David's voice broke. "It's too damn hard. You need to go."

Patrick's jaw tightened. "You've barely spent twenty minutes with her."

"You have to understand." Joanna spoke up. "We lost the most important person in our lives and I heard what you said, that she wouldn't give up the pregnancy. I believe it. Our daughter was headstrong and impulsive from the day she forced her way into this world and almost took me out of it."

A soft sob escaped Joanna's throat. David put his hand on his wife's shoulder and squeezed, and Patrick felt the gesture like a vice grip on his own heart.

"But you were her husband and that little girl out there is just a painful reminder of what we've lost. We don't know her at all." She held up a hand. "Part of that is our fault, I'll accept that blame and carry it with me the rest of my days. But there's blame to be placed at your feet, too. We didn't visit, but we weren't the only ones."

Patrick felt *that* blow as if a three-hundred-pound man was doing CPR on him.

"I know. And I'm sorry. But we're here now."

Joanna turned to stare out the window, the conversation over.

Fine.

Patrick called for Aoife, who came running from out back, the dog at her heels.

"She likes me, Da!" Aoife exclaimed. She didn't need these people in her life if they didn't want to be a part of it. She had folks in her corner and would live a full life in spite of Rachel's parents. At least in Dublin, Aoife had grandparents who adored her.

"And I cleaned up her poop and put it in the rubbish bin. See? I'm ready for a dog, I think."

"You just might be." He had another idea, then. Patrick couldn't force Rachel's parents to love Aoife, but he could give her a life filled with love nonetheless.

"We're grateful you brought our girl home," David said stiffly.

"Of course. Aoife, say goodbye to David and Joanna." He wouldn't call them grandparents if they didn't want the job.

"Bye and thank you. Take good care of my mommy, okay?"

Patrick walked him and Aoife out, stopping just before David slammed the door in his face.

"We'll go, but know this—I won't bring her here again until I hear from you. So think long and hard about what you're giving up. You didn't have a choice with Rachel—she made that decision for all of us, God rest her soul. But you've got a choice now and you're making the wrong one, dammit. You're making the wrong one."

Patrick choked back a ball of heat that had built behind his throat as David shut the door. His eyes watered.

"Are they mad at me?" Aoife asked when they got in the car.

Patrick smiled down at her. He might not have a clue what he was doing raising a sassy little Irish lass, but he'd never let her feel unloved, unappreciated, or like she was an annoyance to be swatted away.

"Nah. How could anyone be mad at you, *mo grá*?"

Aoife scowled. "You were mad at me the other day," she pronounced. When his brows furrowed in confusion, she added, "When I took your lunch and fed it to the ducks."

He chuckled. "Yeah, I was, wasn't I? But that was more hunger, see? A man gets awful like a bear when he's hungry." He threw his head back and roared, then tickled Aoife, who giggled and begged him to stop. "But, Aoife, hear me loud and clear. Those people in there might share your blood, but that doesn't make them family."

"Because family shows up?" she asked, quoting him.

"Yep. Family shows up."

"Does that make Sorcha our family?"

Patrick rubbed his chest where a pressure had begun to build.

"Yeah. I guess it does."

To what degree? A partner? A *spouse*? That he couldn't answer. But he knew one thing for certain.

"Are you okay with me inviting Sorcha to spend the rest of the day with us?" It was a crumb dropped, to see if Aoife picked it up.

Aoife put her hands on her hips, leaned dramatically to one side and said, "Duh."

Oh, boy. He made a silent plea to the fairies to let Aoife's teenage years be easy on him.

Patrick pulled out his phone and dialed. Sorcha picked up on the first ring. "Patrick, hi. I was just thinking about you."

He smiled. "You were?"

"Yes. I'm going through the paperwork and seeing what needs to be tweaked before our board meeting at the end of the week."

"Oh, the trial. Well, I'll let you get back to it." He knew better. She was working, something he both admired and resented in that moment. The lilt in her voice, the way her Irish accent crept in when she was excited…

He wanted to be the cause of that.

"I was thinking of you in other ways, too, you know," she added. His smile returned. God, was he a goner. "So, what's up?"

"Nothing that can't wait," he replied.

"Is that Sorcha? Hi, Sorcha!" Aoife called. Patrick winced.

"Hi, Aoife. Wait, are you not here at the hospital, Patrick?" she asked. "I thought you had a surgery when I left, uh—I'm not on speakerphone, am I?"

"No. You're not."

"Do you need help with her, because I can—"

"I—we—actually came to see David and Joanna."

So we could put that part of our life fully behind us and start our future. With you, I hope.

"Oh."

"Yeah. It went about as well as you can imagine."

"I'm so sorry, Patrick. Aoife probably has so many questions." So did he. "What can I do?"

He closed his eyes, praying she wasn't asking just because of Aoife. He wanted her to ask because *he* mattered to her.

"Actually, I need a favor. Can you meet us at 1222 South Graves?"

The laugh he heard on the other end said she'd figured it out.

"Are you sure about this?" she asked.

"I am. You in?"

"Oh, I wouldn't miss this for the world. Her face will be priceless." Patrick's smile deepened, but thankfully, she couldn't see that, either. "See you there, Quinn."

She hung up and Patrick, eejit that he was, couldn't wipe away the smile that grew each mile he got closer to their destination. Excitement at seeing her and exploring these new blossoming feelings overrode any frustration from earlier.

Despite the inauspicious start to the afternoon, it was sure shaping up to be a good one.

CHAPTER FOURTEEN

SORCHA TOOK ANOTHER PHOTO. It was hard to stop, when Aoife and the new Great Dane puppy were rolling around on the ground, the former laugh-crying with an abundance of joy while the bumbling ball of loose fur and floppy ears lapped up her tears, causing squeals.

"I love him, Da. I love him so much!"

The scene was positively adorable. A rogue wave of emotion crashed against Sorcha's chest when Aoife said, "Thank you, Da, thank you, Sorcha. Thank you, fairies, for making my family complete."

The wave didn't knock her over, though. It merely hit, a splash of water that woke her up and felt… warm. Good. *Nice.*

Which was an understatement compared to what Aoife's father made Sorcha feel. Delicious. Hopeful. *Loved.*

She shivered as his hand brushed against hers. Maybe—

No. It was impossible to expect her worldview to change overnight simply because these two had made her aware of what she'd been putting aside her whole life in order to protect her heart. She cared deeply for Aoife, for Patrick, but they were leaving at the end of the year. And then where would Sorcha be?

Alone, again. Always.

Still… When Patrick grabbed her hand and squeezed, then snapped a selfie with all of them in the frame, she couldn't help but think of her father's saying every time life took a turn he hadn't expected.

Is ait an mac an saol. Life is strange.

It certainly was. Either way, before she and Patrick slipped too cozily between one another's sheets, she should find out when exactly he and Aoife were going back to Dublin. It would be easier if she had a date in mind, and could protect her heart with a plan.

"What's his name?" Patrick asked.

"*I* get to pick?" Aoife asked. Immediately, the tears were gone and excitement took their place. "*Oh, my gosh!* I have so many ideas. But…" She frowned.

"But what?" Sorcha asked.

"But I don't want to make the wrong one. The fairies have been listening to me, which is why I have you for me and my da, and a dog for when you and my da are busy. What if I pick the wrong name and the dog doesn't like me?"

There was the wave again, stronger this time. Sorcha stumbled a bit.

"You won't get it wrong. Let the name come to you, love," Patrick suggested, saving Sorcha from having to respond through trembling lips. "Dogs and people come with a personality, and names that fit. You were always an Aoife. Strong, beautiful, and filled with joy."

"I was?" Patrick nodded and the wave of water rose up Sorcha's chest, with nowhere to go. It was getting hard to breathe.

"You were. Still are. So, what's this little ball of energy called?"

The puppy, as if he was suddenly aware of all eyes on him, put on a show of sniffing around their feet. He was such a curious dog, so filled with joy. He reminded Sorcha of the cartoon and kids' books she'd introduced Aoife to.

"I think his name is George," Aoife announced confidently.

Sorcha couldn't help but laugh. "I just thought the exact same thing."

Aoife's face lit up. "You did?"

"I sure did. Look at him acting like a detective, eager to find out everything he can about us. He's just like—"

"Curious George!" Aoife squealed. She clapped and the noise got the puppy's attention. He bounded over, jumped in her lap, and began kissing her face.

Both Sorcha and Aoife giggled.

Patrick's brows arched. "So, that's it? George?"

"George Floppy McFlopperson Quinn," Aoife announced, erupting into yet another fit of giggles.

"That's quite the birth certificate," Sorcha said. The little girl's happiness was contagious. All Sorcha's misgivings about what had happened the night before evaporated. "You might want to keep it to George when you call his name, though."

"Okay," Aoife agreed. "Maybe I'll call him Georgie sometimes, though?"

"Of course. Nicknames are required for dogs."

"I'd have thought a fairy name would be appropriate," Patrick said, scratching his chin as if he was trying to understand the scene he'd just witnessed.

"Fairy names are for *fairies*, Da." Aoife rolled her eyes and Sorcha bit her bottom lip.

"Well, I like George. It's a strong name, one I don't mind calling out in the park when he runs away." The full weight of his grin had a dizzying effect on her. She reminded herself she was a prominent surgeon who'd just had a prestigious clinical trial funded—and not a teenage girl with a crush.

"True." She smiled.

"How'd you both think of the same name?" he asked as they watched Aoife run off with the puppy. "It's like you two were speaking your own language."

When he wrapped an arm around her shoulders, she marveled at his strength, which seemed to biologically transfer to her when they touched. What might it have been like to face her challenges with the steadfast support Patrick seemed to offer? How much sooner might she have reached her goals?

What new ones might have cropped up along the way?

It was a dangerous line of thinking, especially with how tenuous their future was. But it didn't stop her wondering. That was the power Patrick had over her—he allowed her to dream out loud for the first time in her life.

"It's from the kids' book *Curious George*. Did you ever read it?"

"I can't believe I missed that connection. Well, it fits. Thanks for this. It's nice to see her so happy."

"I'm curious about what happened with David and Joanna," Sorcha said.

Patrick sighed, the fires turning to dull embers. For the first time, she noticed the pain etched in the lines around his eyes. He'd been through so much, too.

"It was awful. They're still so wrapped up in their grief they ignored Aoife. Worse, they asked us to leave before they'd even asked Aoife one question about herself."

A shudder rolled through him, and it didn't take a physician to see how badly he was hurting.

"Give them some time," she said. "Let them grieve and—hopefully, with what I know of them, anyway—they'll come around."

Patrick's muscles tensed. "No. Absolutely not. They blew it. Like hell I'll give them another chance to hurt her."

Sorcha placed both hands on his shoulders.

"I know you don't want her to know any pain,"

she began. "But you can't protect her from every discomfort, either. That's the balance of being a parent. Rachel's folks never understood that, not really."

"Like your parents?" he asked. God, he saw right through her armor, straight to her bleeding heart, didn't he?

"No, they didn't understand, either. Maybe that's why Rachel and I bonded as quickly and deeply as we did."

"So how could I willingly throw Aoife to the wolves again?" Patrick's voice cracked and so did Sorcha's heart. She leaned her forehead against his.

"You don't. You give them time and space to grieve, then you open the lines of communication again."

"And if they don't respond? What then?"

"Then you give them more time and space. There isn't a statute of limitations on love. All I'm saying is, don't give up yet."

"Thank you," he whispered. His breath was warm and inviting on her skin. All she needed to do was lift her chin and she'd be able to claim his mouth with hers. The desire rocked through her like an electric pulse.

"Always."

She wasn't sure who moved first, but his lips met hers, lighter than the night before. He teased them open and traced them with his tongue, more tender than exploratory. She tasted salt as a tear met their mouths, but also a delicious sweetness. If she could survive on that taste alone, she would. Her fingers slid around the base of his head, fisted in his hair.

She wanted this man something fierce. He was uncertainty and disruption but also…*calm*. Sorcha eased into the kiss, deepening it.

Aoife screeched at the same time the large puppy collided with the couch. "Ew! Why are your mouths like that?" The chaos forced Sorcha and Patrick apart as if an explosion had erupted between them.

"Um…" he said, running his hands through the hair Sorcha had just had tangled between her fingers. "We were kissing," he explained. His gaze met Sorcha's and her cheeks warmed with mortification. They'd been caught red-handed doing something that was somewhere between actual kissing and something much…*more*.

"You don't kiss me like that."

Patrick cleared his throat, and Sorcha covered her laugh with a cough.

"No, I don't. When an adult likes another adult as more than a friend, as something special, they sometimes kiss like that."

Sorcha was divided between watching Aoife's grin widen and replaying his words over and over.

Likes another adult as more than a friend… Something special…

Sorcha had never wanted a family, had staved off dating to avoid the complication of caring for another person who had the power to distract her from her one goal—to help children like Cara.

Now she was playing with AED paddles—one

wrong move and she'd kill the life she had mapped out for herself.

Her pager went off, breaking the mood and, thankfully, the tension.

Oh, no.

"What is it?" Patrick asked.

"It's Elsie."

He patted Aoife's head and sent her to get dressed.

"I'll get George settled and let the day care know Aoife is on her way. Meet you there?"

Sorcha nodded. Not needing to explain the urgency to Patrick was such an unexpected gift.

"I'll call ahead to the hospital and let them know we're coming." She ran out the door, her heart racing.

Patrick's scent and taste were still infused in Sorcha's skin, her lips, her hair, but her thoughts were laser-focused on the small patient they'd had on the operating table just days earlier.

She dialed the hospital on the way in, her hands gripping the phone like a lifeline.

The nurse's brief was laced with urgency. Elsie was in a medically induced coma to allow her residual swelling to subside, but when they'd attempted to reverse the effects of the anesthesia, her vitals had plummeted. It had to be an infection, but where?

Another surgery to figure out what was causing the infection was the only option. And it wasn't a good one.

"Please let her be okay," Sorcha whispered as she

tore through the ER doors and sprinted back to the surgical wing.

And let the red tape get cleared on my trial as fast as possible.

That was the only sure way to save children with neuroblastomas. The crippling realization it wouldn't help Elsie, though, seized her chest like a STEMI heart attack. Sorcha barely made it through the scrub in, her vision narrow. Sounds reached her ear canal as if they'd had to travel through the whole Atlantic Ocean first. Her pulse was erratic. She knew the signs. A panic attack. She hadn't had one since she was a child, since the night her sister had passed and her parents had gone to sit vigil at the mortuary, leaving Sorcha alone with neighbors and her grief in her small room. They'd never come back to her. Not emotionally, anyway.

Would Elsie's siblings feel that same sense of loss if their sister died and took their parents' love with her?

Sorcha *had* to fix things. Had to forget about Patrick and keep her focus on what really mattered— saving lives.

But as her breathing became more and more shallow, as her vision clouded black along the edges, she wondered who was going to save *her*?

CHAPTER FIFTEEN

PATRICK PRESSED A HAND to Sorcha's forehead, another on the small of her back.

"I'm okay," she said. "It was a panic attack, I think, but I breathed through it."

"Okay. I'm still here." Her breathing slowed, her shoulders rolled back. When she gazed up at him, he was struck by two things—first, her beauty. He'd known gorgeous women in his time, his wife included. But Sorcha was magnetic, confident, and alluring in a manner that drew him to her in ways he was still figuring out. Even now, sweat dampening her forehead, her eyes wide with terror and pupils dilated, she was the most stunning woman he'd ever laid eyes on.

Which led him to the second thing he'd noted. He brushed her damp hair off her forehead and sat by her side.

I want to take care of her.

Not that she needed him to—which only added to the desire; she didn't rely on anyone, couldn't count on her family or anyone else, so he wanted to be there for her on the days she could do with someone to lean on.

Days like today, when all the independence in the world couldn't keep the worry at bay.

"She'll be okay. We know what we need to do and we got here in time."

Sorcha nodded and took a deep breath. "Thank you. I just—I need this trial to go through. I can't lose any more children or see any more families have to—"

"I know. And it will. Mick is on it."

"I want to believe that, but he mentioned something about red tape and then we got this call about Elsie—"

Patrick squeezed her hands. "It's terrifying, I get it. But it's out of our hands. Right now, the trial isn't as important as helping this patient. Okay?"

"Yes." Sorcha shook her head. "Of course." He held out his hand and she took it. The immediate heat between their hands couldn't be ignored. This woman was his catalyst—whatever the chemical reaction was, he didn't care as much as the way she ignited him. "I'm sorry for breaking down."

"No apologies. But we should get in there sooner rather than later."

Risking a quick glance around, he planted a kiss on her cheek. Not for her, so much as him. But the smile that replaced her earlier frown was a nice ancillary benefit.

Patrick grabbed a tablet from the nurses' station in the ICU and pulled up Elsie's chart.

Sorcha sighed and he let out a low whistle.

"A cerebral edema," Sorcha declared. He nodded his agreement. "A bad one, too. I thought it was an infection."

Patrick pointed to a spot on Elsie's scan. "Me, too. This looks vasogenic, but I can't see where the swelling is coming from."

"Right here," Sorcha said, pointing to an almost invisible gray spot on the image. "The swelling is causing pressure to build up along her ocular nerve. If we don't get in there and relieve it, she'll lose her sight."

"Damn. Did I miss something in her last surgery?" Patrick wondered aloud.

"Not at all. This is a side effect of a traumatic surgery for a juvenile patient. It's why—"

"It's why we need a less invasive option like the trial," he said. She nodded and met his gaze. He understood now, in a way he hadn't until that moment. This singular focus Sorcha had wasn't without purpose. From a medical and scientific standpoint, he'd always known that, but the human component had eluded him. "This is what happened to your sister?"

She nodded again. "She died of complications from the surgery, yes. But the disease would have killed her either way. We simply didn't have the medical advancements we have now."

"Okay, you're on lead with this. Tell me what you need as your second so we can save this little girl."

The situation was fraught with tension, pressure,

and risk. But she smiled. And he knew it would be okay.

Eight hours later, it was, but not without cost. Elsie's surgery was hard on the poor girl's body, and recovery would be a long road for her and family. But, sans an unforeseen complication, she'd get to walk the road not many children with neuroblastomas did. It'd never been more clear why trials like Sorcha's were necessary. All the modern, expensive surgical equipment he'd ordered wasn't going to be half as effective as fixing the problem from within, with a minimally invasive procedure.

Patrick leaned against the sterile walls and let himself slide down to the floor. He pulled down his mask and wiped the sweat from the top of his lip and forehead.

"You did amazing," he said, glancing up at Sorcha, who didn't look as half as fazed as he felt. "I'm going to tell Mick we need to get that red tape shredded, though. I can't keep having marathon sex sessions all night followed by eight-hour surgeries."

Sorcha's cheeks turned an adorable shade of crimson. She glanced around and he laughed.

"It's just us, Sorch. But does that blush mean you're embarrassed about sleeping with me?"

"No," she said, her smile crooked and oh-so-tempting. "But we're at work."

"Duly noted. You should be proud of what you did in there, by the way."

The blush deepened. "Thanks. You, too."

"Can we celebrate tonight?"

She opened her mouth to reply when Patrick's pager went off. He used the sink basin to help him off the floor. *Jeez.* Had he ever been so exhausted?

You didn't exactly get any sleep last night.

And he'd endure it again to have the time with Sorcha, vulnerable and freer than he'd ever seen her. Getting to appreciate that with his hands, his mouth...

"You'd think he had a listening device planted on me so he can reach me just before I'm about to crash."

"Mick?" she asked.

He nodded. "And the board. Must be about the contractor's bid. Mind if I take off and see what they need?"

"Of course not. But, Patrick?"

He turned around.

"I'd love to celebrate with you."

He smiled, the grin reaching all the way past the fear and trepidation, warming his heart.

"Great. I'll see you tonight. I can't wait." And that was the truest thing he'd ever said. He already hated the idea of walking away from her, but duty called.

Mick met him at his office door and gestured him inside, his eyes bright.

"Why do you look like you're up to something?"

"Because I am." Mick winked and Patrick's stomach swished with concern. Mick's plans—stemming back to when the two had known one another in med school—were usually half-hatched...yet too tempting to pass up.

"Tell me why I'm here," Patrick said. "Eight hours on my feet is only fun if it's at a U2 concert."

"Your patient is doing well?"

Patrick shrugged. "She'll live. Let's just say I'm happy about Sorcha's trial that will make invasive procedures like what Elsie went through no longer necessary."

He watched Mick's face, concerned with the half smile his friend gave him.

"Yeah. Anything we can do to help more patients."

Vague and dismissive.

"Is everything okay?" Patrick asked.

The words *Is the trial still on?* were on his lips, but it wasn't his question to ask.

His worry evaporated when Mick's smile broadened.

"Things are fab, friend. As long as you agree to be my permanent CMO."

Patrick exhaled shock. That wasn't what he'd expected.

"What happened to Dr. Collins?"

Mick waved the name off. "Staying home with her infant. She'll be back on the surgical staff next year, but she's decided the chief position is too much to take back on."

Patrick leaned against Mick's desk, his thoughts running wild. It would be a drastic shift for him and Aoife to move their lives to America. Not just for them, but for those who cared about Patrick and his daughter.

His folks would lose access to their granddaughter—at least on a consistent basis.

But… They could always fly out and visit.

"So?" Mick asked, leaning forward, expectant. "What do you say? Want to stay here and work with Dr. Kelly and me?"

Patrick perked up. He would get to work with Sorcha's brilliance each day.

And at night…

He cleared his throat. He'd be an ass if he made this decision so he could continue to sleep with Sorcha Kelly. At the same time, to pretend she wouldn't weigh into the decision would be lying to himself.

It wasn't the sleeping with her he wanted, but starting there and seeing what else was possible. A week ago, would he have thought it was a bad idea? Yeah. At the same time, *everything* had changed in a short amount of time. He hadn't set out to develop feelings for Sorcha; in fact, he considered it a small miracle anything real and substantive had taken root.

But it had. He liked her—a lot.

"I need to talk to Aoife and my folks," he said.

And Sorcha, too.

"See what they think. Aoife's life is in Ireland, and this would be a huge move for her."

Mick raised his hands. "Sure, sure. Of course you do. Get back to me by the weekend?"

"Got it." Patrick tried to keep his voice even. By the end of the weekend? That was three days away; how was he supposed to make such a life-changing decision so quickly?

"But, Patrick? Make no mistake. I want you for this job. You're the best man for it."

Patrick nodded, but his brain winced. He could use some real-life fairies right about now.

The text telling him that Aoife was fed, read to, and in bed warmed his heart at the same time it caused his stomach to drop out. As he made his way to his apartment, he knew that's all he wanted— a family for Aoife, a partner he could share long days and dreams with. Even challenge one another when they needed it. And okay, some spectacular lovemaking wouldn't hurt anything.

But was it too soon to make a major life-changing decision based on a couple great weeks and one sultry night together? It'd been good with Sorcha, really good. But to move here with the hopes that...

That what? She'd want to move in with him and Aoife and continue the happy family routine indefinitely? That they wouldn't get sick of one another, making work and their living situation untenable?

Um...yeah.

He frowned at the sheer audacity of his subconscious. But... It wasn't wrong; that's exactly what he was hoping for.

He got to the front door of his apartment and gazed up at the lit window above. Sorcha was reading in the chair closest to the window, her knees pulled up to her chest. Even from two floors down he could see her bottom lip tucked between her teeth. He knew that look—the book must be at an intense scene to warrant her most focused attention.

And that was it. One word settled in his chest, took root and blossomed all at once.

Home. He was home, much more so than in Dublin. He wanted to know more about the woman upstairs. He wanted to build a life with her, raise Aoife together and make her smile every damn day.

He took the stairs two at a time, desperate to get Sorcha's opinion on it all. Worry at what she would think nipped at his heels with each step.

She must have sensed his roiling emotions when he walked in the door. Frowning, she got up from her chair, the baggy cowl neck sweater falling to midthigh over tights and fuzzy socks. She was adorable, but also…sexy as hell.

"What's wrong? What did Mick say?"

He swallowed hard. The words were simple—*He wants me to stay on.* But the implications were vast and filled with risk, the kind Patrick had avoided since Rachel's death.

"Dr. Collins is leaving her position to stay home with her baby. She'll remain on the surgical staff, but the chief medical officer position is too much with a new family."

What a coward he was—he couldn't even say the most important part. Maybe that meant he wasn't allowed to want it—the family, the full life in America.

The woman.

Sorcha's face was neutral, no doubt waiting for him to continue.

"Mick wants me to take it."

There. That wasn't so hard, was it?

The smile on her face said maybe he'd spent too much time on worrying.

"Wow. That's an incredible honor," she said. He tried on a smile, but it didn't reach his eyes. "Isn't it?"

"It's a lot," he admitted. "An honor, yes, but at the same time it means giving up the life we had in Dublin."

Sorcha gestured to a doll and the pile of American Girl doll accessories. "She'll survive living her best life in America. She'll think the fairies made it possible."

"That's true."

Patrick watched Sorcha's face, not wanting to put any pressure on her, but desperate for a break in the armor to gauge her feelings about him, not the little girl sleeping in her room.

"We get to stay in America?" a small voice squealed from the shadows. Clapping emanated from the same spot.

Okay, so not sleeping as much as spying.

Sorcha shot Patrick a grimace. "Sorry. I checked on her just before you got home and she was fast asleep. The puppy is in your room, though. No way Aoife would go to bed with that little cutie taking the bait each time she dangled her arm over the bed."

He laughed and waved it off, then called Aoife over.

The little girl came out, hands trailing a blanket behind her. "I just wanted water, but then I heard you talking about staying here. Can we?"

Patrick didn't even try to mask his surprise. He'd known his daughter loved it here, but thought he'd need to weigh both sides with her.

"You would really be okay living here forever? Or at least a good while?"

"Yes. I already asked the fairies to think about it, but that was just this morning! I *definitely* think they know I'm here now."

He sat and she crawled up in his lap, wrapping her small arms around his neck. "Will you miss Nan and Pop?"

His parents would miss *them*, that was for certain. But they were retired and he had the discretionary income to pay for them to trade off visits with him and Aoife.

And maybe Sorcha?

His chest swelled with hope. This time, he let it. He'd said goodbye to Rachel, talked to Aoife about the potential for moving, and been offered a job in Boston. With no other barriers in sight, it was as if the universe—aka the fairies—had nudged him in the direction of his heart.

"They can visit," she said. Patrick chuckled at the simplicity of her answer.

He kissed her head and put her on the ground, standing up.

"Fair play. I'll let Mick know in the morning that the Quinns will be sticking around for the foreseeable future. Only if a certain young lady gets to bed before I change my mind." Aoife tore off toward her room, eliciting laughter from the adults. When they were alone, Patrick asked the question that had been plaguing him.

"I want to keep seeing you if we stay. But I don't want to put pressure on you, either. Would it be okay to take what happened last night and expand on it?"

Sorcha nodded, her eyes damp.

"What's wrong, *mo grá*?" He cupped her cheek, desperate to kiss away the hurt that seemed etched around her eyes.

"Nothing. I'm just… I've never had anyone ask my opinions before, not about something this big. It's…nice."

Tangling both hands in her curls, he pulled her toward him and pressed his lips to hers.

"Then it looks like I'm meeting with a Realtor tomorrow to talk about selling my place in Dublin."

"And you're *sure* you're happy about that?" she asked.

"Oh, very. Accept that I'm here to do more of this." He kissed her shoulder. "And this." His lips grazed the nape of her neck. "And much more of this." He tipped her chin up and kissed her. His teeth playfully bit down on her bottom lip, sending a surge of longing straight to her core.

When he pulled back, her lips were swollen.

"I guess I could get used to that."

So could Patrick. For the first time in years, he saw a future that wasn't solely based on survival. He saw happiness, fulfillment, and passion, and Sorcha in the middle of it all. Maybe it was too soon—after all, they'd only slept together the one night—but he didn't care. He was going to do everything in his power to help her see a bright future of her own, and maybe, with a little fairy magic, she'd see Patrick as part of it.

With one more kiss, he laughed and picked Sorcha up over his shoulder, carrying her to his bedroom. Who'd have thought that the combination of an intoxicating woman, a sassy four-year-old, and a rambunctious puppy would have him so optimistic he'd put his stock in Irish folklore instead of science?

Only one thing was scientifically proven about Patrick's situation—he was smitten and it would take a cataclysmic event to change that.

CHAPTER SIXTEEN

SORCHA UNDID HER PONYTAIL and shook out the tension that had built at the back of her skull. Pressing her fingers to the bridge of her nose, she inhaled deeply. The faint scent of antiseptic singed the inside of her nose, but it was such a familiar smell, it didn't rile her the way it used to.

A glance at her schedule brought back the tension.

All surgeries. No meetings about the trial, the funding, or even a whisper of when she could move the research out of the lab and into the world. She set down the beaker she'd been using, and it cracked along the bottom.

She winced. Under the split glass was the name of her co-surgeon on most of the patient cases.

Patrick Quinn.

Her boss, colleague, and...and what? She hadn't figured out a title to give him. Boyfriend seemed too cheesy, but anything else scared the willies out of her.

Because...

He's staying in Boston.

She tossed the beaker in the glass recycling and went to retrieve a new one. The news that Patrick was staying was nearly two weeks old at this point, the contract signed, sealed, and delivered, but she still hadn't digested it. Maybe couldn't was closer to the truth. If she did, she'd be forced to reckon with two nagging questions.

Is he staying for me?

He'd denied as much, but if they broke up, would he resent her for giving up his house, his career in Dublin, his daughter's life back home?

Her second question was worse, somehow.

Am I willing to do the same for him?

It was not as if she'd been unclear; he knew how important the trial was to her. It was *everything*.

The guilt ate at her, but not solely because of Patrick's decision to stay.

Sorcha usually went home after him, but the gap between their departure times was shrinking week by week. She reasoned that it was because all she needed to do for her trial was wait for the red tape to clear, but the truth was…more complicated.

I want to be at home with him. I want to cook, laugh, and build a life with him.

More than complete her trial? She wasn't sure, nor was she certain it mattered. She could want two things at the same time, couldn't she?

Maybe it would be easier to figure out her feelings if the trial was going anywhere.

A knock on the lab door startled her.

She walked to the door, tentatively opening it.

As it always did when she saw Patrick, her breath stalled in her chest. Today, he wore a button-down fern-green shirt that brought out the flecks of gold in his emerald eyes. The shirt was fitted, rolled up along his strong forearms, with the top two buttons undone, showing a hint of his muscled chest.

Sorcha swallowed. "Hey, you," she said. "I thought we were meeting for lunch?"

"It's nearly two."

She grimaced. "I was in my head, I guess."

His smile disarmed her.

"I figured as much. That's why I come bearing treats," he said, holding up a paper bag. "I brought you a soft pretzel."

"You're a god," she said, her hand itching to tear the bag out of his grasp. Luckily, she didn't have to; he surrendered it with a peck on her cheek. If this was what a relationship was, she could handle it.

"A god, hmm?" He leaned in, nuzzling her neck, and her stomach roared with desire, hungry for something other than the pretzel in her hand. When he nibbled her earlobe, a flash of heat flooded the sensitive area just south of her abdomen. "Well, why don't we close the door and I'll show you just how godlike I can be."

She might've moaned, but then she shook her head. "Not here. Mick might swing by with news about the trial." Or so she could hope.

Her desire for both—work and time with Patrick—was a push and pull between her head and heart.

"Fair enough. Mind if I hang with you while you eat? I've got some time to kill before I pick Aoife up from day care."

Sorcha tore into the pretzel, ravenous all of a sudden. "Of course. Sorry I didn't come down to meet you. My alarm rang, but I thought it was for the sample."

Patrick waved her off. "How'd the sample perform?"

"The same. Perfect. I just feel like I'm wasting time now. Have you heard anything?"

Patrick shook his head and ripped off a small section of pretzel. She threw him a "you only get one of those" glance and he laughed. "Nothing from Mick, though I'd imagine you'll hear before me."

She nodded, cleaning up her station as she finished off her lunch. It had barely made a dent in her hunger.

"Wait," she said, realizing that Patrick picking Aoife up meant he was done for the day. "Why are you off so early?" she asked.

"I'm taking Aoife to see the Celtics play. Remember? You set it up for us last week."

"Oh, my gosh. And I told you I'd come—"

"Shh. You have work. It's fine. I can manage this little excursion."

"But… You hate basketball."

"How am I supposed to like something with half the excitement of Gaelic football and athletes that are paid more than I'll see in a lifetime? Though *she* thinks—"

"The fairies talk to the leprechauns," Sorcha said. He nodded, a grin as wide as the River Shannon making her heart thump a little louder.

How strange that this man made her long for her home country at the same time he made her feel like his apartment downtown was home.

"You know, we parlayed your tickets into a sky-box thanks to some donor from the board who Aoife accosted after she saw his Celtics hat." He kissed her, his unasked question between their lips.

Would she consider joining them?

Sorcha looked at the lab. Her space was cleaned up, not that anyone else would care. There was no word on her trial, the surgical schedule was empty the rest of the afternoon, and besides, Mick could call if he needed her.

What did she have to lose?

You've never left in the middle of the day. Ever.

Well, maybe it was time she did.

Her brain quieted while her heart rejoiced.

"I'd love to. If you're sure Aoife wouldn't mind me hijacking her daughter-daddy date."

Patrick leaned in and kissed her square on the mouth.

"Not at all. I would have reminded you about it sooner, but I didn't want you to feel pressured to leave work early."

That's the thing, though. She didn't feel pressure from him. Just care, comfort, and passion. It made the choice easier than it should've been.

"To be honest, it'll help distract me until I hear something from Mick. I'm going crazy."

That half-truth was better than what her heart whispered: *I like you and will go anywhere you ask.*

Patrick took her satchel and slung it over his shoulder. "I'll distract you any time you need it, *mo grá.*"

He held out an arm for her to take and she did, marveling at how biologically responsive her body was to his. As a scientist, she was so curious about the bond she shared with a man she'd sworn to hate for eternity. As a woman, she was curious about very…*different* things.

She was curious about the feel of his strength wrapped around her at night and how much stronger it made her. About the way his lips on hers ignited a fire in her chest, but still sent goose bumps across her skin. About what the indentation of their bodies on his pillowtop mattress said about how her dreams were changing.

"For now, a basketball game sounds nice."

Disregarding the sun high in the sky and the sound of her office door shutting while people still scurried around them, she decided to simply enjoy the day rather than worry about what she *should* be doing, or what was the point of leaving in the first place?

Two hours later, she, Patrick, and Aoife were on their feet, screaming at the top of their lungs at something Sorcha had no clue about. Only that the rest of people in the box were up in arms, waving at the refs as if they could be heard over the rest of the stadium's din.

"C'mon, ref!" Patrick shouted, his accent strong as ever. "That wasn't a foul. Je—"

"Da-a-a!" Aoife said, a frown on her face. "You're not allowed to say that. No bad words, remember?" She crossed her arms over her chest, and Sorcha stifled a giggle.

"I do," Patrick said. Aoife went back to the game and he grimaced. *"Cailín's* got me wrapped around her finger, doesn't she?" he asked Sorcha.

"That's an understatement. Hey, I'm going to grab a diet soda. Can I bring you something back?"

"The same. Thanks, hon."

Sorcha nodded and walked toward the bar before Patrick noticed the red on her cheeks. They'd slept together, woken up naked beside one another, but somehow hearing the pet name in public reeked of intimacy. Not that she minded...

She waited in line, caught up in a small fight under the Celtics' basket that had broken out.

"Quite a game, isn't it?"

Sorcha pulled her gaze from the court. "Um, yes." She smiled at the gentleman from their box in front of her, shaking her head. "Whew. That was only the first half and it was so exciting. I don't know how you do this every week and don't all succumb to massive heart episodes."

The man laughed. "My wife wonders the same thing. She says board meetings aren't this stressful."

"She's not kidding. I'm Sorcha, by the way."

"Harold. My wife is on the hospital board."

"Nice to meet you."

"Your daughter seemed to be having a great time," he commented. Sorcha glanced at Aoife, who was smiling and animatedly talking to Patrick and a woman—Harold's wife, she realized. Sorcha caught something about Aoife's whole list being granted thanks to her dad and his special friend. She grinned, pride blossoming in her chest until—

"Oh," she said, her cheeks burning. Harold might not have realized it, but Sorcha had fully let herself live in the fantasy that Patrick and Aoife *were* her family. "She's not my daughter. I'm just…friends with her dad."

What else could she say?

"Is he the doc that might move over here from Ireland?"

Might? Sorcha let the word roll off her back. Maybe Harold wasn't privy to the inner workings of the hospital board.

"Sure is. He's brilliant and we're lucky to have him."

Harold nibbled on the inside of his cheek as if he was thinking. "That must make you the surgeon who presented the neuroblastoma trial, then."

Surprised, Sorcha nodded. "I am. Your wife told you about it?"

"She did, but, uh, only in passing, of course." Harold's smile faltered. "Anyway, nice to meet you," he added.

Patrick met Sorcha's gaze and frowned.

Everything okay? he mouthed from across the skybox.

She shrugged, finally given her turn at the bar. She got the sodas but took her time walking back to Patrick. Sorcha didn't have much interaction with others in social settings, but the way Harold had walked away after mention of her clinical trial didn't sit right.

A beeping in the room got her attention. She followed the sound to Patrick.

"It's an emergency. Bus accident with Boston University's track team. They need a trauma-trained surgeon and I'm all they've got that's close. Dammit."

"Da," Aoife warned. He patted her on the head.

"Do you mind?" he asked, nodding down at his daughter.

Sorcha took Aoife's hand. "Not at all. Do you need me to come in with you, though?"

Patrick shook his head. "Mick didn't say as much, but keep your phone on you."

"Will do."

"Thanks, Sorch. You're the best." His mouth stayed open, like he wanted to add something, but then he just kissed her instead.

Patrick left after kissing Aoife too, and Sorcha felt the overwhelming urge to text and ask him to check in with Mick about her trial after the emergency passed. There was something going on, and she needed to find out what. But putting her boyfriend on the case? Yeah, that was messier than when he'd just been her boss.

Had she made a mistake mixing pleasure with work? God, she hoped not.

But in that moment, Aoife's hand in hers, she knew—she'd crossed a line somehow and couldn't go back.

CHAPTER SEVENTEEN

PATRICK SLID HIS MASK down around his neck. "Wow!" he exclaimed, wiping his brow. "That was a brutal surgery."

The operating lights in the surgical suite were dimmed while the cleaning staff came in. The crimson splashes of blood on the floor were a pattern of near loss that, even when it was mopped up, left an indelible mark. And it was a pattern that could be avoided with non-invasive procedures.

The world needed more Sorchas, more doctors willing to put ingenuity and research above personal glory, more doctors willing to research instead of only cut.

Mick whistled. "It was a close one. But it brought back memories, didn't it? We were the surgical studs of medical school."

Patrick chuckled and threw his paper towel at Mick.

"Surgical studs? I don't know about that."

"Don't forget the fun we used to have just because you paired off with Rachel the minute you landed back stateside. We'd pull off surgeries twice as long and then hit the bar like we just woke up. Those were the good ole days."

"I don't know," Patrick said, watching the blood and antiseptic cleaner funnel down the drain, wiping the slate clean for the next surgery. Would it be needed, or something that an innovative doctor like Sorcha could have fixed with a little time spent researching other methods? "I'm starting to wonder if Sorcha is onto something."

"What do you mean?" Mick asked.

"Her trial for neuroblastomas has me thinking about small cell carcinomas and TBIs. Maybe I'll build off her research and see if I can get the trial extended to other similar traumas. It would do a helluva lot of good, wouldn't it? To save kids like that—" he pointed to the ICU room where the patient had been moved "—without the trauma to their bodies... It would change lives."

Mick sighed, ripping his mask off and tossing it. "Patrick, we need to talk."

The unease that settled low in his chest made him anxious. "What's up, Mick?"

His old mentor wouldn't meet his eyes, instead making a big show about gathering his lab coat, his wallet, and his keys from his personal locker. "Let's go grab a cuppa at the café across the street," he said.

"Mick," Patrick said through gritted teeth, "you've got three seconds to tell me what's going on before I go back to my girlfriend and daughter."

Mick at least had the grace to look at Patrick

when he sighed, resignation in his eyes. "There's a problem with the hospital's funding. We need to make cuts."

Patrick's world slowed to a stop. He could hear his pulse keeping time—*thump, thump, thump*—the way he'd been able to in medical school when extreme focus was warranted, when his scalpel was paused above a malignant mass. He'd already put his house on the market, despite a warning from his parents to wait, to make sure his contract went through before he pulled a massive trigger like that.

Never in a million years did he think he'd have to call them a mere couple weeks later and tell them they were right, that his offer had been pulled.

"Explain in detail, Mick, and don't leave a damned thing out."

"Fine," Mick said. "But remember I'm just the messenger."

Patrick didn't say a word. His arms crossed over his chest, frustration and worry brewing below the surface of his skin.

"You know we've been struggling to finance the rest of the new oncology floor," Mick started. "That equipment you chose—"

"That you approved," Patrick added, though his pulse kicked up a notch.

Mick nodded. "Well, it tipped the scales and we're in trouble."

"So…"

"The board came up with three solutions and voted Monday night."

"I'm just hearing about this now?" Patrick asked incredulously. "Well, what did they decide?"

"They're using the funding the hospital set aside for the neuroblastoma trial." Any relief Patrick felt that his job was safe was short-lived.

Sorcha's trial. Her life's work.

"It's just temporary—a two- or three-year hold on all trials until we're back on track financially," Mick added hastily.

"Find it somewhere else. You can't cancel Sorcha's trial, Mick."

"That isn't the only place we're restructuring. We've had to make some hard, deep cuts to make things right."

His frustration from earlier blended with horror, resulting in anger. Deep, rolling anger. This was Patrick's fault. "Are you saying if I'd chosen different, cheaper equipment for the oncology floor—"

"We'd still be in trouble. Just not as bad."

"You can't do this," Patrick growled. "She's worked too damn hard and for far too long to have it taken from her now."

Mick's chin dropped to his chest. "This surgical wing is the part of the hospital we need the most. It covers us financially when other departments fall short—I mean, elective surgeries alone will account for—"

"Elective surgeries?" Patrick hissed. "You're cutting a proven lifesaving new treatment plan, a protocol that will save hundreds of children's lives, for nips and tucks on people who have more money

than sense?" He stood, shaking with rage at the unfairness of it all.

"Jeez, man. Don't act like you haven't had to make hard calls like this in the past."

"I haven't. I *wouldn't*." And his hospital in Dublin never would have made him.

"Look, this isn't ideal—" Patrick shot Mick a warning glance that hopefully conveyed how much more than "not ideal" this was. He seemed to get the message. "But it isn't that we're canceling the trial altogether. We're just moving it back until we can refill the coffers."

"You said *years*?"

Mick had the audacity to *shrug*. Like this was just a minor inconvenience for him. "I don't know, to be honest. No one is scrambling to donate to big, corporate hospitals anymore."

"I wonder why," Patrick mumbled. He raked his hands through his hair and across his jaw. Was it just hours ago he was with Sorcha and Aoife, laughing and cheering on a sports team? And now the world as she'd created it was about to crumble around her. "She's gonna be crushed. I hate that I have to ruin her night with this."

Mick's eyes went wide and he stood straighter. "You can't tell her, Patrick. I'm sharing this with you in confidence as the CMO. But it's the board's responsibility for legal reasons to outline the shift in dates and approval. We're scheduling a meeting to let her know at the end of the week."

Everything became crystal clear, as if time had

stilled, offering a slo-mo play-by-play of the past few weeks. Mick's distance. His appointment of Patrick as CMO. The odd look he'd seen on Sorcha's face as she'd talked to that board member's husband at the game.

"How long have you known?" he growled. Patrick's tone was even, but even he heard the threat coating the words.

"We've been in danger for a couple weeks, which you knew, to a degree." Patrick's brows shot up. He opened his mouth to annihilate his supposed best friend, but Mick kept talking. "But it was just Monday that we—they—voted."

"That's why you brought me on full time, isn't it?"

Mick shook his head. "I brought you on because you're the best man for the job—and I thought you could be objective about this. I'm sorry, Patrick, I really am."

"So, what? I'm supposed to go home and lie to her? She's practically living with me."

"No," Mick said. "You just go on and keep your work life separate from your personal one. I know you can do that."

The warning in Patrick's eyes turned molten.

"Don't you dare bring Rachel into this."

"I'm not. But this is messy with no easy way to fix it. We've both been there before is all I'm saying."

Patrick paced the small, sterile room.

"Why can't we close up the half of the floor that isn't finished yet and—"

"There's no way the inspectors will allow us to function in a half-finished space. It presents all kinds of health hazards."

"I'm well aware. I'm not suggesting we hang a tarp and call it good. I'm just saying there's got to be a way to fix this that doesn't lead to us terminating the most promising project this hospital's ever had." Mick's brows rose. Patrick pointed a finger at him. "And this *is* me being objective. That trial is brilliant and you know it."

"I do," Mick said. He pushed open the doors to the sanitizing room and looked back. "I'm upset about it, and if there was anything I could do to save it, I would. But unless you can magically find ten million dollars, it's over. The best you can do is help see this construction project through and then, down the line, help Dr. Kelly get the trial back on track."

Mick walked out, leaving Patrick alone in the still, quiet darkness. Normally, with a daughter, puppy, and girlfriend he cared about deeply all waiting for him at home, he'd follow after Mick and sprint till they were all safe and happy in his arms.

That was before he'd been told he'd have to wreck at least one—but perhaps both—of their worlds. He dialed his folks to see if they'd contact his Realtor in a couple hours when the Irish business world opened.

"Hey, Ma," he said when her voice came on the line. "How're you and the old man?"

"Patrick! Oh, darlin', it's good to hear your voice. We're doing well. Your father is like a new man now that he's retired. Says his goal is to be good craic and make a naughty name for himself in the village."

Patrick chuckled, but his heart was heavy. It was being pulled between three places, stretched too thin to imagine he was getting out of this unscathed.

"That sounds like Da."

"You'll like to hear the idea he had the other day."

"Oh, yeah?" Patrick threw the phone on speaker and set it down so he could press the heels of his palms against his eyes. Pressure and heat built up and he knew an eruption was close.

"He wants to come over to see ya. Not for a couple weeks, mind you, but maybe get a small cottage outside the city so we can live half the year with you and Aoife. What do you think about that? I didn't even have to hint at it."

"Aw, Ma. That sounds perfect." And it did. The tears still fell, though, hot and heavy.

"*Mo grá*, what're you hiding from me? Somethin's wrong, isn't it?"

His mother's voice reached across time and distance and acted like a balm on his bleeding heart. She knew him too well.

"It is." He filled her in and at the end of it, only silence met him on the other end.

"Oh, my. That's a tough one."

A cough. His mam must have put him on speaker at some point. "Hey, Da."

"Real poxy jam you're in, son."

"Yeah." What else could he say? It sucked. He wanted to tell Sorcha what was happening, but how could he without making things worse at the hospital? "Sure is. And I don't have a clue what to do, either."

Because what did he care about the hospital or his role as the CMO when Sorcha was about to lose everything?

"There's no way to get the money from somewhere else?" his mam asked. "Some other hospital?"

"Jeezus, Mary Kate. Doncha think Patrick would've thought of that already?"

"Well, jeez, maybe he—"

"No," Patrick said.

But...

Unless you can magically find ten million dollars, Mick had said.

"You're a genius, Ma."

"See, Tom? Patrick says I'm a genius. And he's a doctor, so he knows a thing or two about that."

"I'll call you guys soon, but could you please ask the agency to hold off on any more showings? I'd rather not deal with the nonsense until I get things figured out on this end."

"Don't worry, son. We've got you covered."

"Thanks," Patrick said. "I mean it. If I was there, I'd kiss ya both." His mam giggled and even his dad let loose a chuckle. "And thanks for thinking about moving out here. It means more than ya know."

"Of course," they said in unison. He hung up and got to work calling everyone he knew.

Lucky for him—Irish lucky—he had a few tricks up his sleeve yet.

CHAPTER EIGHTEEN

SORCHA TURNED ON the water, her hands rolling over her skin as she shed the baggy T-shirt—Patrick's T-shirt—she'd worn between bed and the shower.

She wished she had more of her own clothes at Patrick's place, but it was too soon for that. Even if she did look forward to coming home to Patrick and Aoife. George, too. The latter two would bound up to her, matching energy and noise volumes, stories to tell about their days together. It was safe to say Aoife and the rapidly growing puppy were in love with one another.

Speaking of love—or something close enough to it that it scared Sorcha senseless—Patrick met her each day with a deep kiss, a glass of wine or tea depending on some algorithm he'd designed around her mood. Wildly enough, he hadn't gotten it wrong yet. They all ate dinner as a family, Patrick's hand on her thigh, then she got Aoife ready for bed while he cleaned up. Each evening, they read Aoife a story together, save the couple nights one of them would be called in for an emergency surgery. Once Aoife was tucked in snug-as-a-bug-in-a-rug—a holdover from Sorcha's childhood she'd recalled and implemented—Patrick would whisk Sorcha away for a bout of lovemaking that was both toe-curling and heart-pounding. Sorcha couldn't remember the last night she'd spent at her apartment.

How was she supposed to keep concentrating on work when *after* work felt so good?

She rinsed her hair and turned off the water.

More troubling? Patrick and Aoife, the life they represented, had begun to feel like *home*.

A *family*.

Which was fine. Dreams changed and grew according to one's courage. But Sorcha had bucked against the idea of a family for one reason—they could be taken from her without any notice, a heartache she didn't think she'd survive twice.

On the surface, Patrick leaving her seemed impossible. As smitten as she was, he seemed worse. He always reached for her hand when they were out walking, sat next to her at staff meetings, kissed her when she least expected it, including at work.

But something nagged at her brain, making it impossible for her heart to fully let go.

Each time she'd inquired about the house in Dublin, he'd tell her it was still on the market, but that there weren't any hits. That alone wouldn't ping any flags, but in the beginning, his phone had blown up with house showing requests that had suddenly stopped earlier in the week. And ever since the basketball game, a shadow passed over his face each time she mentioned work, the expansion of the surgical wing, or how frustrating it was not to know anything about the trial yet.

It wasn't that she didn't trust him, but she'd begun to suspect he wasn't being honest with her about something.

Ask, then.

Her subconscious was meddlesome that morning, wasn't it?

Start with asking if he's still okay selling his house.

If he wasn't, she'd listen to why and they'd work through it. Because he was showing her in every other way that he was there for her. Every way that counted.

Still...

"Hey, Patrick?" she called from the bathroom as she layered on green eyeshadow. O'Shanahan's pub was having an Un-Patty's Day party, and it was the first time she and Patrick were getting a sitter to go out alone. It was nice getting ready as a couple, tucking Aoife in and reading her a book—about fairies, of course—together. One united front.

"Yes, love?"

Her stomach warmed at the moniker. They hadn't said they loved one another yet, but each time he called her "love" her heart screamed that it wanted to say it back. But if—when—she did, she wanted it to be *safe*. With no reservations or odd feelings. Nothing that could creep up and snatch away the sense of security she'd tucked around her like a blanket.

She walked out of the bathroom and let loose an audible gasp. Patrick sat on the edge of bed, shirtless. Each carefully defined muscle was on display; his biceps flexed as he slid on socks and the loafers he'd picked out. He was an Adonis, a biologically perfect specimen. And his thousand-watt smile was aimed at *her*. A flash of red-hot lust *almost* burned away her question.

"Can I ask you something?" She walked over to him, hoping proximity equaled courage.

"Always. But only if you take that towel off and get into bed. I want to answer whatever you're curious about with my mouth on your—"

"The sitter will be here in minutes," she argued, cutting him off with a finger over his lips. Which she regretted with every fiber of her body. Even though Mick had put a meeting on the books for the next day—hopefully to sign the trial paperwork—and they had this party to go to tonight, she'd be lying if she said she wasn't already looking forward to coming home later with Patrick.

Home.

He kissed the tips of her fingers, drawing one into his mouth and sucking on it.

"Fine. What's on that pretty, intelligent mind of yours?"

Her heart, actually, but she didn't correct him.

"I was wondering how your house sale is going back in Dublin. You haven't mentioned it recently."

The familiar shadow crossed his face, but it was

gone so quick, Sorcha wondered if she'd imagined it.

Yet the pause in his answer was the same as other times she'd been brushed off.

He didn't meet her gaze when he finally answered. "I asked my folks to reach out to the agent and pause the sale for now. There's a downturn in the market, so I'll try again in a couple months when it's safer."

Sorcha's head and heart both issued pings of warning, and it took every cell in her body to calm the tremor in her voice. "Oh, I'm sorry to hear that. Just a downturn in the market? You're sure nothing else is the matter?"

He nodded, but his smile seemed forced. Her stomach flipped. Was it just her past, a lifetime of parents who didn't show up for her, that warned her of danger anywhere real feelings were involved, or was there an actual problem? She hated that she couldn't trust her own gut.

"Yep. Now get over here and let me kiss you while I button my shirt."

Sorcha obliged, letting the warmth and safety of Patrick's lips flush out the cold that had settled low in her chest. When his shirt was buttoned, she grabbed her own top—emerald lace with a sheer tank underneath—and slipped it on. His eyes followed her every movement. God, it was sexy having a man as alluring as Patrick watching her dress.

Patrick's cell phone buzzed on the table. He glanced at it, but then his gaze went right back to her. She felt it as if it were his hands and not his eyes tracing her body.

"This view never gets old. Real estate agents would make a killing if they just implanted you into every bedroom, putting on shoes and drying your hair, and—"

She stopped him with a kiss. "You're ridiculous. I look like a drowned rat."

"My drowned rat." He sat at the edge of the bed and pulled her on top of him, nibbling at the base of her neck. She squealed with delight. He knew just how to make her squirm in all the best ways.

His phone buzzed again and he flipped it over, ignoring it.

"Do you need to get that?"

He shook his head before diving into the crook of her neck, teasing her earlobe with his tongue. She wasn't sure if the goose bumps were a result of Patrick's seduction or a manifestation of her fears that he was hiding something.

When he patted her on the backside and gave her the space to finish getting ready without distraction, she decided maybe she'd just let it go and enjoy her night. All she wanted was to relax into this man and let him love three decades of neglect away.

Half an hour later, they were on the back roads of Boston, avoiding the I-93 at all costs. With the elevated train down for maintenance, Patrick had argued driving was the best option. He'd said since this was their first real date, he wanted to "pick her up."

It wasn't going well.

Patrick's knuckles turned white as he gripped the steering wheel tighter.

"Are you okay? I can drive if you're not comfortable—"

"I'm fine. It's the same as driving in downtown Dublin, just on the other side of the road."

"And car."

"Yeah, that." His jaw clenched. She swallowed a giggle, supposing she'd feel the same if the roles were reversed and she was carting them around downtown Dublin.

His phone was hooked up to his car radio and Glen Hansard, her favorite Irish singer and songwriter, crooned over the speakers. Patrick stiffened as traffic stalled.

"We're fine. We've got plenty of time." She put a hand on his knee and his shoulders relaxed. She loved that she had the power to calm him with a simple touch. Heck, she loved him, period. Why had that been so hard to admit?

Because you're not sure why he's being so evasive all of a sudden?

True, but she was sure of *him*, and that was all that mattered.

"Does anyone use their indicators in America?"

Sorcha laughed, swallowing it when Patrick's brows pulled tight in the middle of his forehead. This man was the most competent surgeon she knew, and yet he was a nervous wreck in evening traffic. The disparity made him human, made him real to her. Made her heart beat a little faster, too.

"Um…hon, we call them turn signals. Or directionals."

"Well, they should be on, whatever they are. I mean—"

"Patrick?" she interrupted. He kept his eyes on the road, still tense, despite the smile he shot her.

"Yes, love?"

"I love you. I know this isn't really the time or place, but—"

He crept up to the stoplight, threw the car in park and leaned over, grabbing her cheeks and kissing her.

"Shh… It's perfect." He kissed her again. "In fact it's the only thing worth braving this mob of eejits for. I love you, too, Sorcha."

They sat there, grinning at one another until a car honked behind them. They laughed as he put the car in drive and inched forward.

"I've been wanting to tell you for a week now," she admitted, her cheeks flushed with emotion.

He pretended to scoff as they passed the bar, Patrick scanning the road for a parallel parking spot.

"Is that all? Wow. I don't know if I should be offended or…" He made a show of putting a hand on his chest as he backed into a spot two blocks away from O'Shanahan's. "I've known since the minute you and Aoife waved madly at each other across the room while I accepted this position the first time."

"You did not love me then," she said. But that

didn't stop the loud thump of her heart as it swelled against her rib cage. "You'd just met me."

"Ah, but I did." She giggled, but was silenced with another kiss, this one deeper, more rife with meaning. "A woman so fiercely dedicated to her work, but who still finds time to chase fairies with my daughter?" Another kiss. "An Irish lass who kisses like she was born to do it? And who wants to save the world with the same passion? I'm head over heels, Sorch."

He kissed her again, and Sorcha didn't know how her body could contain all the happiness welling up inside her. If this was what love felt like, she chastised herself for avoiding it all these years.

"Why didn't you say anything sooner?" she asked.

"Ah, love. Would you have been ready to hear it?" he asked.

She shook her head. "Probably not. I mean, I think if I'm being honest I've felt it as long as you, but I don't have much experience in believing in love or family."

Patrick leaned in and kissed her, his forehead resting against hers.

"I hope you start, love. Because we'll have all that and more and anyone who tells us we're off with the fairies, we'll kick their backsides and prove them wrong."

He tangled his hands in her hair and kissed her yet again, teasing her lips open with his tongue. He tasted like peppermint, which sent Sorcha into

overdrive. Lust *and* love? It was almost too good
to be true.

"Do we have to go in?" she mumbled against
his lips.

"Nah. I'm sure those folks headed to the theatre
would be right as rain if I take this fine *ting* and
make love to her on the boot of the car."

She giggled, about to lay into him about being
medical professionals and all when his phone
chimed again. This time, the text came through on
her dash, since his phone was connected.

Hi, hon. You didn't answer my last text, but I have
today on my calendar as the day of the meeting.
I hope it went well and she's okay. Love ya, Ma.

Sorcha sat back against her chair, her lips still
swollen from kissing.

"What is this?" she asked. Her pulse raced when
he bit his bottom lip and frowned.

"Dammit," he muttered.

"What the hell is going on? And don't lie to me,
Patrick."

"There's a snag with the trial," he whispered. She
barely heard him over the music.

"A snag?" Her chest constricted, making it hard
to breathe. "What kind of snag?"

"I'm not allowed to say more, Sorcha. Mick
said—"

She let out a humorless bark of laughter. "I don't
care what Mick said or didn't say. I'm asking *you*."

She shut off the radio and squared up to Patrick. He met her gaze, but what she saw there wasn't love. No, it was loss—*that* was a look she recognized.

The silence was punctuated by his deep inhale and exhale before he spoke.

"They're taking the money and moving it to the surgical wing expansion." He must have seen the way her cheeks drained of blood, heard the gasp that escaped her mouth. "Just for now. He promised they'd reallocate the funds and that your trial is first up when they do, Sorcha, but—"

"Is he coming tonight?"

"Mick? Yeah, but—"

Sorcha didn't wait for Patrick to stop her, to defend something as indefensible as knowing about this and keeping it from her. She stormed out of the car and ran toward the bar, the threat to her future—and the whiskey she'd have to consume if it was ripped from her—pushing her forward.

CHAPTER NINETEEN

"DAMMIT." PATRICK UNDID the seat belt before attempting to chase after Sorcha. He ignored the traffic whizzing by him and ran toward O'Shanahan's.

Breathless, he caught up to Sorcha two doors before the bar.

"Sorcha, stop. Please."

Tears streamed down her face, and any trace of the love-infused grin from earlier was replaced with pain. Her lips twisted into a scowl, her eyes wide and red.

"How could you keep this from me?"

He froze. It was a question that had plagued him every waking hour of the past few days and some of his nonwaking hours, too.

"Mick told me I couldn't tell you for legal reasons, so I tried to work on it from my end. I can fix this, Sorcha."

"That's not your job as my boyfriend. Honesty is."

"And as your boss?" He winced at the hurt on her face.

"Are you saying I have to pick between your roles

in my life? If you make me make that choice, I will, but you won't like it."

"Sorcha, I'm sorry. I thought I had it handled."

"Rubbish. You were scared. You took part in covering this up because you were terrified about what my response would be."

Was that what had happened? It stung like the truth dragged over raw skin.

Patrick held her gaze. "The board voted, not me."

"But you could have told me."

He raked his hands through his hair, down his cheeks, which bore three days' worth of stubble. This had been killing him, too. Didn't she see that?

"I couldn't. The money isn't there for a trial this year, Sorcha, and we won't have an oncology floor in the surgical wing at all if we don't finish the renovation."

Sorcha's fingers trembled. She was furious and he didn't blame her. He was, too. Which was why he'd been working his butt off to get new funding, funding the hospital couldn't touch. If she could only see...

"If we don't get this trial, we'll lose more patients than any improved surgical suite will save in its lifetime."

He'd thought the same thing after Elsie's surgery. And somehow, he'd let the politics of the job sway his actions and hid the news from Sorcha.

"I know. I'm sorry, Sorcha. You have no idea how much. But if you'll just hear me out—"

"You want me to *listen*? To what? More excuses?" Her eyes didn't soften at his lame attempt at an apology. If anything, her gaze hardened like scarred skin after an injury. "Maybe if you'd told me straightaway—"

"Sorcha, I swear I'm this close to securing your trial funding forever."

"Are you staying in Boston?" she asked.

"Of course. I mean, I want to."

"Is the Dublin house really on pause until the market turns, or are you scared of being caught between Mick and me and needing a place to run to when everyone's lies catch up to them?"

He balked, his voice suddenly stuck on the sliotar ball-sized guilt lodged in his throat. She wasn't pulling any punches, was she? They didn't bounce off, either. They landed—*hard.*

"I—I don't know." If he didn't have Sorcha, and the job was going to be more of the same—him being used as a political pawn rather than being part of lifesaving surgeries, what was the point? "I pulled it because of this news, yes, but only so I could concentrate on the money, on getting it back."

Her laugh was without a hint of humor. "You weren't committed to staying for my sake, or it wouldn't have mattered, Patrick. Don't you think I recognize a family with one foot out the door?" He opened his mouth, a rebuttal at the ready. That's not what had happened, although he could see why she thought it was. She cut him off with an icy glare. "And even if that wasn't true, you *lied* to me. That isn't love, Patrick. Not even close."

God. After all she'd been through, he'd taken her trust and squashed it.

"I'm sorry, Sorcha. I wasn't lying when I said I wanted to move here, when I said I loved you. I hid the reason I paused the house sale because I knew you'd read into it, and I didn't want you distracted from working on the trial. When the time was right and the money came through, I wanted us to be ready. That's all it was."

"I can't believe we're here again. I've already told you—you don't get to decide how I read into things. It's your job as my partner to talk to me. *Especially* when it's hard."

"I'm not your parents, Sorcha. I'm not out to leave you or neglect you. I just… I just wanted you to have it all."

Patrick ignored the furtive glances of people heading into the Irish pub as they walked past the fighting couple.

"I *had* it all," she whispered. "I let you in, Patrick, despite my fears. I fell in love with you and your daughter and trusted that you wouldn't ever put me in the position my parents did when they froze me out, made unilateral decisions about our family without me."

"That's not what I did."

But didn't you?

Her glare said his subconscious wasn't far from the truth. Again.

"And what about you?" he asked.

Wait. No. This isn't the way to go. Don't get defensive.

He'd had enough truth, enough judgment. He'd messed up, yes, but he'd been trying to do the right thing. Didn't that count for something?

"What *about* me?" Her voice was cold, a steel scalpel's edge.

Fear flooded his circulatory system. Panic seized his chest. But his brain couldn't reach his heart in time to stop it from dumping his feelings all over her. "You keep me at arm's length and I'm willing to bet you wouldn't consider leaving Boston for me. But I'm expected to get it all right the first time I upend my and my daughter's lives?"

She took a step back as if she'd been slapped.

"No. That's not what I'm asking and you know it. I just wanted you to talk to me. I've discussed my parents with you. How I can be there for you and Aoife even though nobody showed me how. I might have been buried in my work, a little closed off, but I worked every day to let you and Aoife in, despite my worry you'd do the same thing to me that my parents did."

Her sniffle punctuating the end of her sentence implied *and you did.*

He grasped her hand, which trembled. "I know. And I appreciate everything you do for us. But do you realize you tell Aoife more about your past than you tell me? Look, I just wanted time to sort this out."

"How dare you talk to me about opening up

more? It takes two, you know. I've asked you—twice—not to try to fix things for me. I don't need a white knight. I need a *partner*."

Her tears had abated, but what replaced them—an icy calm—wasn't any better. He was losing her, and he couldn't let that happen. Not when he'd only just found out what love could look like, feel like.

Patrick groaned and leaned on the brick building. "I wasn't trying to be a white knight. I just wanted to make it right. As your colleague. Or boss, or whatever."

"The waters were muddled since we're dating, so it isn't totally your fault. But as a partner, you kept it from me." A shudder rolled through her, and he wished he could kiss her hurt away. "Maybe you're right. We're both still keeping each other at arm's length… It's got to mean something, and if I hadn't been so distracted by how good it felt to be with you, I might have noticed it sooner."

"What are you saying?" he whispered.

"I'm saying we had a good time, that I'm grateful to you for teaching me how to care for more than just my work, but that it was always going to be too complicated to work in the long run."

"You're giving up on us?" The jovial music coming from the bar and the laughter of the people inside was jarring—the wrong soundtrack for the scene.

He knew he could fix this, find the place the bleeding stemmed from and cauterize it. Couldn't he?

"What's there to give up?"

Patrick's heart was racing too erratically, his blood pumping too fast. He was losing control. "Sorcha, I know I messed up. I should have come to you no matter what Mick said. But please give me a chance to make it up to you."

For the briefest of moments, it looked like he'd said the right thing, stopped the bleeding. But the calm gave way to a sadness so profound, it was worse than death.

"I know why you did it," she admitted. Her lip was drawn between her teeth, but not because she was deliriously happy or focused on her novel like at home. Her voice quivered. He hated it—that she felt anything other than trusted, desired, loved, and in control of her life. "You were right. I *am* closed off. And my relationship with my parents is complicated at best. But I let you in. And Aoife. I gave you two time I could have spent working because you mattered to me. You mattered more than the rest. I... I just need time to think about everything."

He'd been a coward, afraid to let anyone in lest they break his and his daughter's hearts. Maybe that's why he hadn't gone to her with the truth, hadn't trusted that they could find a way to fix it together. Rachel hadn't let him be part of the solution when she'd been handed down her diagnosis, but Sorcha...

Sorcha wasn't Rachel.

His fears were well-founded, yes, but life wasn't going to just keep throwing beautiful, incredible opportunities in his lap. He needed to do the work if he expected the reward.

Patrick took her hand in his. "Then take the time you need. But don't push me out, Sorcha. I want to help you heal that relationship with your parents, as well as make the rest of your dreams come true."

"It's not your job," she whispered. "Maybe it never was. I didn't need someone to make my dreams come true for me. I only needed you to support me while I did that for myself."

He was nodding like he agreed with any of this, like they were already in the bar, celebrating Un-Patty's Day.

Before he could step out of that dream and into reality, Sorcha was walking toward a taxi, leaving him with the sound of an Irish drinking song to drown his misery. His impulse was to run after her again, to make this right if he had to suture every damned bleeder with rudimentary stitches until they healed.

Over the music, he heard a whisper.

Let her go. Find a way to show her the truth and then go to her.

Damn if a chill didn't slither up his spine and root at the base of his skull.

He hadn't had any whiskey he could blame it on, but he would have sworn the voice was one of Aoife's fairies. Maybe his daughter was onto something, thinking there was a force bigger than him guiding the way.

Patrick shook his head and headed into the bar to give Mick a heads-up.

He only hoped the voice—whatever it was—was right because watching Sorcha turn the corner out of sight, thinking it was the last time he'd held her, loved her, was enough to make him think he'd never be okay again.

CHAPTER TWENTY

SORCHA ROLLED OVER and glared at her beeping alarm clock. She unearthed a hand from the mountain of pity covers she'd burrowed under the previous night and snoozed it. Her bed moaned as she rolled back into the nook she'd made for herself, only an eye-sized peephole to look out.

The view was as bleak as the feeling that had led to the blanket fort in the first place. She found fault in every aspect she could see of her own apartment. The laundry basket in the corner was out of place—Patrick's basket nestled in the closet was much more efficient. Then there was the matter of her bedroom layout. The bed faced away from the window, which was fine and dandy if she didn't need a strong solar influence to motivate her on early mornings. But it also meant on rainy days—like that morning for example—she couldn't peer out at the gray landscape and use it as an excuse to stay cozy in her bed.

The most glaring fault with her apartment was its small bed and one bedroom. It meant there wasn't anyone beside her to kiss her awake, to snuggle against when the rain batted against the panes of glass behind her. There wasn't any padding of six little feet sprinting toward her from the back room, primed to jump into the middle of the blankets and beg to join her.

No Patrick. No Aoife. No George.

And it was all her fault.

The alarm rang loudly against the wall of cotton she'd erected. This time, she turned it off.

The silence wasn't any better, nor was the gentle urging of her mind to get up, get out of the house, and get to work.

"What's the point?" she mumbled. The trial was all but dead—the meeting to go over the details postponed by Mick until today—her relationship with her boss was fractured on both a personal and professional level, and her heart was broken. Patrick had messed up by not telling her about the trial, sure.

But something he'd said that night at the bar two weeks ago had nagged at her every time her mind quieted. Which, since she'd moved out of Patrick's apartment and taken herself off all his surgeries, was a lot.

I'm expected to get it all right the first time I upend my and my daughter's lives? he'd wondered.

No, that wasn't reasonable.

In the moment, she'd thought, *Well, yeah, for something this big, you should have done better.*

But every morning she awoke alone, every successful surgery where she turned around and found no one to celebrate the success with, she'd realized the truth. He'd done what he had to help her in the best way he knew how.

It wasn't perfect, but when the scalpel was put to skin the first time, it was rarely a clean cut. It took practice. All good things did.

It'd taken losing him to realize another hard-won truth—she wanted the risk that came with a family and love if it also meant experiencing the joy and fulfillment that accompanied them. Having Patrick and Aoife and losing them certainly shone a light on each and every error of her ways.

With a frustrated *harrumph*, Sorcha slid out of bed and went through her morning routine. Not that she liked a single moment of her solo shower, single bagel in the toaster, or the sole coffee mug that would sustain another long day, alone.

How did I live this way for so many years?

When she got to the hospital parking lot, she froze, unable to leave the car.

There, walking from the entrance, were Patrick, Aoife, and George. Maybe she could inch out to the back lot without them seeing her...

"Guess not," she muttered when Aoife noticed her and waved enthusiastically, drawing Patrick's attention. "I'll make it quick, and it'll be like they weren't here at all."

Her heart argued otherwise. She'd missed those three like a body in the desert missed water, but seeing them there, at work, might drown her instead of bringing her back to life.

She made her way to the family, her eyes carefully pinned to Aoife and the puppy so she didn't have to meet Patrick's gaze. Even so, she could still feel it sliding over her, pleasant and warm.

"Sorcha!" Aoife exclaimed. "I missed you."

"Oh, Aoife. I missed you, too." Flashes of heat burned behind Sorcha's eyes. "What's this guy doing in the hospital?" she asked.

George's eyes lit with recognition, but at a small cough from Aoife, he held back from bounding up to her. Sorcha was impressed with his training and size in just a few short weeks. He must've gained twenty pounds of solid muscle since Sorcha last saw him.

"We're training him to be a servant dog," Aoife said, her chest puffed with pride.

Sorcha glanced up at Patrick for clarification and was hit with the full force of the beauty of the man. His million-watt smile that could power an OR, the scruff on his chin she wanted to rake her hands across, the crinkle around his bright eyes when they were in on the same joke.

"A *service* dog," Patrick whispered to Sorcha, adding a conspiratorial wink. For a brief moment, she allowed herself to believe things were back to where they were, that they were a family. Her chest ached beneath her rib cage. "He had his emotional service certification today so he can volunteer in the peds wing from time to time as a therapy dog."

"Got it," she whispered back with a wink. "Aoife,

that's such a great idea. It'll help George and the patients, and you."

"Dad said I couldn't be a doctor yet, but I was old enough for this. Someday I wanna help people like you do, Sorcha."

Okay, forget a dull ache. Her chest threatened to split down her spine.

"And you'll make a wonderful physician. Until then, you and George are going to be quite popular here."

Aoife hugged Sorcha's leg.

"Guess what, Sorcha?"

"What's that?" Sorcha wanted nothing more than for that little girl to hold on forever. On one hand, it was impossible having these small interactions with a child she'd hoped to help raise, but on the other, at least she had this. Not seeing her at all would have been catastrophic.

"Grandma Jo and Grandpa Dave met George," she announced, patting the dog that was now equal to her in height. In another month, the darling girl would be able to ride him like a pony.

"Is that right?" George gave a brief bark as if to say "yes."

"What a good boy. So, what did they think of George?"

"Well, I dunno, because we had to leave to take Da to work, but I think they loved him. Right, Georgie-Porgie?" She skipped away, George at her side, only a brief hop betraying him as the puppy he still was.

"They asked us to take him home after he knocked over three new pots of rhododendrons with his tail." Sorcha laughed. God, she missed Patrick. In time, she'd grow to appreciate the brief drive-bys of her almost-family, but right now, she hurt. "He won't be invited back, but at least we will be. They're joining us for a Celtics game next week."

"I'm so glad you mended those fences, Patrick. I really am."

He trailed a hand down her forearm until it reached hers, and then squeezed it once before dropping it. A shiver of awareness raced across her skin.

"We've got a long way to go yet, but the bridge is under construction at least, thanks to you. I was ready to tell 'em to get lost, but you showed me what Aoife would lose out on. Thank you, Sorcha."

She cleared her throat, which was suddenly thick and lined with heat. "Um...of course."

"I know I don't have any right to ask you this, but would you be open to doing the same with your folks?" he asked. "Not that it's any of my business right now, you know, what with..." He trailed off.

She nodded before an answer had fully formed in her head. "Yes, I would be. I can't give out that advice if I'm not willing to take it, and for the first time in my life, I feel like I'm ready. And I have you to thank for that, too."

"I guess we weren't all bad for one another," Patrick said. He rocked back on his heels. Was he nervous?

"No," Sorcha admitted. "We weren't."

"Anyway, I'm glad. I hope... I hope you can forgive your folks."

"I already have. I'm not mad about things anymore. Not about anything," she added. His eyes sparkled with understanding. "Life is too short and people mess up. But those who matter deserve another chance to learn from their mistakes, and also to hear about what they were doing well, too."

"They do?" The obvious hope in his voice buoyed her.

"Mmm-hmm. There isn't much that can't be forgiven when it comes to the ones we love. Especially when it was done with the best of intentions. Sometimes, emotions just run hot when there's something important at stake and—"

"And people say or do things they wish they could take back." He finished the sentence for her.

"Exactly." It was obvious they weren't just talking about her parents anymore, but where did they go from there? "I'm sorry, Patrick," she finally said.

"Me, too." The two words cracked down the middle.

"Will I see you at the meeting later?" Getting a call from Mick last night was the only reason she was in on a Saturday. Maybe at one point she'd have been there anyway, but that had changed the minute she realized there was so much more to life than working. Even if the work meant a lot to her, what good was it to give others their lives back, only to lose her own in the process?

She had Patrick to thank for that, too. And

Aoife… Even Mick and the board had helped in their own way. The pulling of her funding and subsequent loss of what she'd thought was the most important thing in her life had led to a *real* loss, one she might never get over.

Her family. Patrick, Aoife, and George.

"You sure will." The sparkle in his eye made her pulse quicken. Why did he look so happy to be there on a weekend? "I'm just dropping these two off at the day care. Save me a seat?"

She nodded and made herself a promise—she would *not* read into Patrick's words. Hope was a fine thing to have, but false hope? Well, she knew better than anyone how fatal it could be.

No, she'd just be his friend and hope that someday he could forgive her for bailing on him for making a silly mistake. She'd blown his trust, and it was up to her to build it back.

She would, even if it took as long as she'd been working on her research.

Sorcha made her way to the boardroom, not surprised she'd beaten everyone there. She had half an hour to kill so she scrolled through her email, deleting the junk and answering some from other hospitals she'd put feelers out to. She wasn't looking to move, but maybe there was a place she could sell the research, get the trial going again at least.

One email caught her attention. It was from her mom and the subject read Long overdue. Her pulse racing, she clicked it open.

Hiya, hon...

Sorcha choked out a small sob. She could hear the Irish greeting in her mom's brogue and she'd always thought it would break her, but it didn't. It was a healing salve, cooling a long-ago burn.

I wanted to start the conversation I should have had with you years ago. I love you, and I'm, oh, so sorry. I should have been a better mother. But that's neither here nor there anymore. I will be better, from here on out.

Sorcha chuckled and another hiccupped cry escaped.

I know it may be too late, but can we meet to talk? I hear you're up to some amazing things, and I want to know about them. I want to know about you, hon. You know my number, and I'll wait for you to reach out.

Sorcha responded.

Yes. I'd love that. I'll call you.

Then she closed the email, but only after reading it three more times, chewing on each word, savoring it, and swallowing it into her heart.

It couldn't be a coincidence that her mom had written today, after Patrick had asked Sorcha if she was open to talking to her parents. It'd been years since they'd talked. And how did her mom know about the work she'd done at Boston General?

She didn't get time to answer the questions because her phone rang.

"Hello?"

"Dr. Kelly, there was a change in venue. Can you come to the new floor in the surgical wing?"

"Of course. I'll be right—" The phone clicked off on the other end. "*Down.* Good talking to you, too, Mick," she mumbled.

She'd think through her mom's motivation in emailing her once the trial postponement was finalized. Why Mick had put it off so long when they all knew the outcome was beyond her.

She got up and made her way to the Thieves' Deck, which was what she called the oncology floor since it had stolen around ten million dollars of funding for something she'd spent a lifetime on.

Of course Mick would want to meet there to show it off. Jerk.

She walked around the corner, grumbling to herself, and stopped short. There, in front of her, was what looked like the entire surgical staff. Nurses and surgeons in scrubs, even the off-duty docs in plain clothes. At the center were Patrick and Aoife, Mick behind them.

"What's going on?" she asked. Patrick nodded above them. She followed his gaze and gasped. Her hand flew to her mouth just as the tears fell.

The Cara Kelly Oncology Center.

"What is this? Patrick? What—"

"I think there are other people who want to explain. I'll jump in at my part." Patrick pulled back Aoife—who couldn't stop bouncing on her toes—and somehow, the tears fell harder. Her mom and dad were there, smiling through their own tears.

"Someone, please. I... I don't understand."

Her mom crossed under the new sign, and Sorcha took a few hesitant steps toward her. They met in the middle and before she could overthink about how to react, her mom wrapped her in an embrace.

"Mo grá..."

"Hi, Mom. I missed you."

"I missed you, too. We both did." Sorcha gazed up through the tears at her dad beside them.

"Dad, Mom. It's so good to see you, but why are you here? Now?"

Sorcha nodded to the group of people waiting with bated breath as they watched the exchange. It was too public, too personal. She wanted everyone to disappear so she could have this moment with her folks all to herself. Well, maybe with Patrick and Aoife, if the circumstances were different.

"We donated the money to finish the build under one condition."

"What money? What condition?"

"When your sister passed, a tycoon in Dublin reached out to us," her dad chimed in. "He'd lost his daughter the same way and wanted to help. We were so lost in our grief, as you know. But we saved the money, put it in a trust in Cara's name, and it just grew over the years."

"I never knew," she whispered.

"We never found the right way to tell you, not when we'd made our relationship so fraught. To be honest, we were just mired in grief and hospitals weren't on the front of our minds."

"Until now," her dad said.

Her mom smiled up at Cara's name.

"Yes, until now. Until you and your work brought us back to what matters most. Family."

"I love it. It's perfect." And it was. But… "How did you know about the build in the first place?"

Her parents both looked back at Patrick.

"I guess this is my cue," he said. He and Aoife joined them. "I told them. Not specifically about the new floor, but about you, your work and why it mattered so much to you. In the beginning, I just wanted them to know what I was up to, but then they volunteered the donation, and it sorta solved everything. Except me not talking to you. That ends today."

Sorcha's emotions were all over the place. Joy at this moment she'd never expected to feel. Confusion at so much new information. Pride in seeing her sister's name above the door of the new center.

"What were you up to? I feel like I've been kept in the dark."

Patrick took her hands in his.

"That was never my intention. I wanted to get out of your way and put you in contact with people who could actually help."

She nodded. "Thank you. Patrick, I'm so sorry

for running out on you on Un-St. Patty's Day. I don't mind you being in my way so long as you talk to me while you're there."

"I'm glad to hear that." He took a deep breath and glanced at her parents. They nodded so he continued. "The good news is, all but two hospitals want to talk to you, meaning if you agree, the trial can start tomorrow and will be fully funded. It will also be in as many hospitals as you want to oversee, with a staff of your choosing."

Sorcha's breath stalled in her lungs.

"How? Why?" Then, glancing at Mick. "And you're okay with this?"

"If it solves our problem and makes it possible to pursue your dreams, of course I am. I never meant to hurt you, Sorcha. I was only trying to save the hospital. Forgive me?"

She nodded toward Cara's name.

"This is a good start," she said.

"It is," he agreed. "And I'll work to rebuild the trust I broke. I fully support this venture. We couldn't have done it without your folks, though. Their donation, coupled with the other hospitals' investments, covered more than we needed and allowed us to take the first batch of trial patients pro bono."

"Like I proposed," she whispered. Patrick nodded.

"Can I call them?"

Patrick laughed. "We invited the first round of participants here for the unveiling of the new center they will be staying in as you work to heal them. Want to tell them in person?"

Sorcha glanced around at the nurses, doctors, and her people. She'd kept everyone away for so long, but no matter what happened with Patrick, she could finally see that she already had what she'd secretly always wanted.

A family.

"I do."

"Good," Patrick said. "We were hoping you'd say that. So, get to work, folks, and give us a minute."

The crowd dissipated, everyone filing away to stations and rooms that would save lives. And she would be a part of it. Happiness threatened to overwhelm her.

When they'd all left, save Patrick, Aoife, and her parents, she exhaled.

"This is amazing," she said. "Thank you. All of you. I don't know what to say."

"Say yes!" Aoife exclaimed.

Sorcha chuckled. "Oh, I already did. This opportunity is too great to pass up. I think I'll need a few days to realize I'm not dreaming, but I'm definitely saying yes."

"Did you already ask her, Da?" Aoife asked. Sorcha's parents grinned at her, gesturing for Aoife to join them.

When she looked back, Patrick was on one knee in front of her.

"Patrick, what are you... You've already done so much."

"And I'm not done yet."

"You don't have to—"

"None of what I've done is because I have to, Sorcha. *You're* what I want, what I need, and what Aoife loves with all her heart. So only tell me no if you don't want me—not because you think my intentions are for any reason other than I love you."

Her face turned as red as the stethoscope band around her neck. "You... You still love me?" she asked. Her lips quivered.

"I've known from the day I met you in the bar and you almost threw your drink in my face."

She laughed. "I didn't—" He quirked a brow. "Okay. If it wasn't good whiskey, I might have."

He joined her, laughing. "Sorcha, from that moment, I knew you would challenge me, that anyone who earned your favor would have to deserve it every day for the rest of their lives. And Aoife reminded me of something the other day."

"What's that?" Sorcha asked. She sniffed, tears of pure joy falling. She didn't bother wiping them.

"That the fairies brought you to us," Aoife said.

"And we don't turn away gifts the fairies bring, do we?" Patrick asked.

"Nope." Aoife stuck out her chin, grinning. "So ask her, Da!"

"I am, I am," he laughed, taking a small box from his pocket. "Sorcha, will you do me the honor of practicing medicine alongside me, raising this little hellion with me, and letting me learn how to love you two ladies for the rest of our lives?"

"Will you marry us?" Aoife asked.

Sorcha looked at Aoife first. "I'd love that," she said. Aoife whooped and hugged Sorcha's parents, who squeezed her back. "Patrick," Sorcha said, turning back to her beloved. "I am so glad I met you, that you fought to get behind my barriers and made this life possible. Yes, I'll marry you both."

Everyone celebrated under the sign showing her sister's name.

"Now, who's ready to go save some lives?"

Everyone raised their hands and Sorcha laughed. The road ahead was bound to have some bumps, but with these wonderful people at her side, she knew she never had to worry about being left behind again.

* * * * *

*If you enjoyed this story,
check out these other great reads
from Kristine Lynn*

Their Six-Month Marriage Ruse
Accidentally Dating His Boss
Brought Together by His Baby

All available now!